Stone Captive

Gwydion Royce

ORACLE OF LOST PATHS BOOKS

Cover Design by Damonza.com

1st edition 2024

Oracle of Lost Paths Books

author@gwydionroyce.com

979-8-9902074-8-6 (eBook)

979-8-9902074-9-3 (Paperback)

CHAPTER ONE

Meg

I knew we wouldn't hit the mark as soon as we left the cabin. In order to keep the binding on the Hounds, I had to split my concentration as I opened the portal. I slipped us into time, but lost focus, so when we landed in the middle of a dirty street, in a puddle of water, in front of a horse and cart with a furious driver, surrounded by a gaggle of bystanders... let's just say it wasn't my best day.

Andrus threw himself over me as the horse's hooves came crashing down right next to us. I stared at the cracked front hoof that had landed only an inch from my head.

The driver jumped off the cart, still swearing, and already calling for a constable, but his concern wasn't for us. People pressed in around us to get a look at what had just appeared out of thin air. To them it would've seemed like a blank patch of street with a giant puddle miraculously produced three people, one of who was very bloody.

Andrus stayed hovering above me, scanning our surroundings for threats. Tension ran thick through our bond.

"Where do we need to go?" he whispered.

"I was aiming for the cathedral," I said. He moved to let me sit up and look around, still crowding close just in case.

Around me was the medieval version of Paris, and life was grim. Waste filled the gutters. Homes crowded close together on the narrow city streets. The smell was heinous. The barnyard odor of the horse that was frothing at the mouth and stomping the ground in agitation provided relief from the stench of unwashed bodies, rot, and every kind of unsavory thing imaginable.

I rolled Gareth to the side when I realized he was lying face down in the puddle of gods knew what. Our clothes were covered in mud, but at least that worked in our favor. It somewhat occluded the fact that we weren't from around here, but I could hear the whispers that something strange was happening.

And these people didn't like it.

"Let's move," said Andrus, holding out his hand and helping me to my feet. He grabbed Gareth, who was almost as tall as him, and packed with far more muscle, and tossed him over his shoulder in a fireman's carry. "We can figure out where to go once we reach somewhere a little safer."

The crowd didn't part readily. Several men tried to stand in our way, and we had to shove through. Nothing surprises burly men as much as a small woman pushing them easily aside. Gods, I loved my enhanced strength. Excited calls and shouts in the distance told me the authorities had shown up and people were wasting no time pointing them in our direction.

"Do you think the Hounds will follow quickly?" Andrus asked.

"I don't know. It's not the same kind of travel that the Ætherim do. They aren't just sliding into past versions of themselves. They're actually traveling independently through time, just like we are."

I had no way of knowing when Bel had put them on our scent, so I had no way of knowing how long it took them to track us to Norway. Now we were all the way across the European continent and 500 years in the past.

"I'm really getting sick of running," I said, frustrated that once again someone had caught us on the back foot. Andrus had the right idea about going on offense.

As we ducked into an alley, shutters from an overhead apartment banged open, and I heard the slosh of a bucket right before I shoved back against the wall to avoid the cascade of waste flying toward the ground.

I tried not to wretch as it splashed at my feet, but a glimpse of Andrus's face made me laugh, despite everything else.

He stared at me, horrified. "At least in my time we knew that if it smelled bad, it needed to be outside the city walls."

A few of the children from the crowd caught up to us and gave chase, calling back to our pursuers about our location. Andrus whirled around and bared his fangs with a vicious hiss. The children squeaked with fright, and one of them started crying as they ran away, yelling for their parents.

"That'll teach 'em," I said, not able to hide my smirk.

After our escape from Athens, I gained a whole new appreciation for running across rooftops. I thought maybe that would work again here, but most of these roofs were gabled and peaked at a ridiculous angle. Pretty sure I saw a pigeon lose its footing and tumble off the side.

We slowed our pace to a quick walk instead of a run, and I had a little more time to get my bearings. We were in the right city. This wasn't another instance of being waylaid in the trap of Bel's cronies. And there was a constant thrumming at the edge of my consciousness that signaled one of the Six.

When I first located the Desma, the only man I had a solid impression of was Arthur because I took the time to check him out. And then when Gareth back-traced our connection, I got a great preview of him as well. But with the others, I had no idea what I was looking for. Not a name, a description, a shoe size—nothing.

Not taking the chance when I had it to look closely was biting me in the ass right now. But I was being drawn toward one landmark. All roads led to Notre-Dame.

"I really wish we could get onto a roof." I tripped over a pile of straw lying in the street and went sprawling.

Andrus bent to help me up, but I waved him off. He appraised the surrounding rooftops and found something he liked, pausing underneath a rickety four-story structure that didn't look like it would hold up to a rough sneeze. A small balcony hung on the side, the shabby wooden door leading out to it standing wide open.

The roof on this building was a little more sloped, so it wouldn't be as precarious to gain purchase once resting on it. But how he intended to get up there was beyond me.

He'd sensed my doubt. "Have some faith in me," he said with a cocky sideways smile.

The crowd gained on us as they renewed their courage with numbers. Andrus squatted down, shifting Gareth, so that his weight was evenly distributed. His thighs bunched as he prepared to jump. I opened my mouth to protest, anticipating both of them falling, but I'd barely formed the words when he leaped into the air and grabbed on to the railing.

We both cursed. He caught the base of the railing and not the upper handrail, so he was hanging fifty feet off the ground with Gareth dangling helplessly on his shoulder.

"Meg, a little help please."

I wasn't sure I could make that jump either, but I didn't have a choice. Andrus looked down and saw what I was intending to do. I backed up a few paces, giving myself room for a running start.

"Wait, you don't have to—"

I sprinted forward, kicking off a barrel tipped over in the alley and using that to add that bit of extra momentum. I soared upward at a much higher speed than I expected, overshooting the balcony and half landing on the roof, hitting dead center of my chest. It knocked the air out of me with a giant *whoosh* and I saw stars for a minute before I slid down, landing on the balcony floor.

Andrus had laughter in his voice when he asked, "Are you all right?"

"Peachy," I said, struggling to my knees and reaching over the edge. The crowd was drawing closer, and their shouts were more keyed up than before. Any minute now, they would turn a corner and see exactly where we'd gone.

I reached my arms through the bars and pulled Gareth to me, holding around his chest until Andrus could climb over.

Gareth groaned as his weight was shifted. Andrus leaped over the balcony railing and hauled our unconscious wolf to safety, humming thoughtfully. "At least we know he's in there."

"Small consolation as that is right now," I said. There was movement from inside the small apartment and beyond the shoddy wooden door I could see someone rustling under the threadbare covers on a straw-filled cot. A racking cough filled the room, and I thanked our lucky stars that we weren't susceptible to plague. I hopped up on the roof edge and Andrus followed, dragging Gareth behind him.

We backed off from the roof's edge and crept around to the other side of the gable, just as the angry voices turned the corner down the alleyway we'd just left. I stayed low and observed the city around us.

I'd only been to the modern-day city of Paris once. The family that raised me had dragged me along to the equivalent of the Met Gala for prominent underworld families. They dressed me up, slapped makeup on my face, and made it clear under threat of being locked away in my room forever that if I stepped out of line and did anything other than sit still and look pretty, there would be hell to pay.

They wanted their showpiece, their key to ruling their own territory once I'd freed the Titans, to be on full display, making them the envy of every other family there. Unfortunately for them, I'd always been the contrary sort, and at that point I'd been under their thumb for almost thirty years. Their threats and abuses didn't scare me anymore. My hatred for them and the Titans outweighed the fear.

The event was in the catacombs—because apparently they love clichés—and I took it upon myself to go on a tour of the tunnels with the eldest son of their biggest rival family.

We'd then turned an ossuary into a real bone room, making sure we were within earshot of some of the most gossipy servants. My punishment had been severe, but their embarrassment had been worse. So it was a win-win in my mind.

"So what are we looking for?" asked Andrus.

I best described what I thought the cathedral would look like at this point in history and we both began to scan the horizon. The mob was still circling, fanning out, and for a moment it was quiet.

This side of the roof was slipperier, and in my shoes, I had a hard time getting purchase. Recent rains mixed with ash and dirt had formed a greasy film. I could tell Andrus was struggling with his footing with the added weight of Gareth on his shoulders. I was already looking for a way down when I stepped wrong and went shooting off the edge of the roof.

"Meg!" Andrus yelled, reaching for me, missing, and sliding toward the edge. My foot caught on the lip of the roof and set me tumbling through the air. My mouth was open in a silent scream as I prepared to hit the ground. A fall from that height wouldn't kill me, but it was definitely gonna hurt. I came to a halt with a jerk that thrashed my head backward and I grit my teeth against the whiplash, wondering what I'd hit.

I opened my eyes just a crack and peaked around. I was floating in midair. The minute I realized it, I fell the rest of the way, splashing into a puddle with a cry of surprise.

I looked up to Andrus. He'd managed to grab on to something and keep Gareth from falling, but he was still dangling from the ledge and part of it began to tear away under the added weight. Any minute it was going to give way and they'd come crashing to the ground. Andrus would be fine, but I didn't know about Gareth.

There wasn't time to think about what just happened and I could hear more people approaching. I leaped to my feet, water cascading off me, and jumped.

Landing was a little smoother this time, and I found a small divot to hook my foot into as I leaned over to drag Gareth back up onto the roof.

Andrus gave me a thankful smile as he flexed his hands, refreshing his grip. "I will never let him live it down that he was unconscious for this long and I had to carry him all over the damn city," said Andrus, trying to catch his breath.

Crawling forward on my hands and knees, I moved around to the other side of the roof. There it was. Notre-Dame cathedral, not yet blackened with age and with brand new flying buttresses on the outer foundations.

I crawled back over to Andrus. "It's north from here. Maybe six blocks away?"

"Six?" Andrus blew out a breath. "If we're going to travel that far, we need to wake his ass up."

I laughed. "Where did you learn that phrasing?"

He raised his eyebrows. "What do you mean?"

I made quotation marks in the air with my hands. "Wake his ass up?"

Only once he'd thought about it did it seem odd to him, and I felt a certain amount of unease through the bond. "I guess I don't know."

I smiled. "I'm sure you picked it up from me. The 'language lexicon.' One more benefit of the bond. Just don't start talking about twerking in medieval France. People might look at us funny."

He mouthed the word *twerking* before his eyes lit up as he realized what it was. "Show me later?" he asked.

"Count on it."

Gareth's breathing was still steady, like no part of him realized he'd almost fallen to his possible death twice. I reached deeper into our connection, trying to find the reason that he was still out. Most of his body was healed. The worst of the damage done was three puncture wounds near vital organs, one in his chest and two in his abdomen.

Then I found it. The Hounds had put a block in place that kept him unconscious. I wrapped my magick around it and slowly spun it backward, unraveling it before I dissolved it entirely. Why would they have gone to the trouble of knocking him out if they planned to kill us?

I placed my hand on his chest and leaned in, speaking into his ear. "You need to come back to us."

There was a stirring of recognition and Gareth groaned.

"Gareth, wake up," I said, stroking his chest.

A small smile worked its way to his face as he reached that border between waking and sleep. I leaned in so close that my lips touched his ear. "If you don't wake up, Andrus might punch you in the face."

He took a deep breath and opened his eyes. "No need for that."

"It's about time," said Andrus, helping him sit up before slapping him on the back.

"Where are we?" asked Gareth, looking around in confusion.

"Paris. 1398."

"And I thought some of the hill forts back home smelled bad." He pulled a face.

Andrus laughed. "That's not even the worst of it, my friend. Just wait until you're on the ground."

"Wonderful."

"Do you think you're able to move?" I asked.

He nodded. "Aye, I'm alright."

The crowd, sans torches and pitchforks, were still circling the alleys below us. "We need to get over there," I said, pointing in the direction of the cathedral. "And the citizen's brigade will be none too happy to see us."

"That does pose a problem," said Gareth. He was stretching and rolling his shoulders, trying to work out the knots. "Were you dragging me around?" he asked, looking sideways at Andrus.

"I could've swung you from your balls, and you wouldn't have noticed," said Andrus. "Just be glad I didn't let you fall or leave you behind."

I snickered as they went back and forth until Andrus got the final word and they dropped it.

"Can you portal us there?" asked Gareth.

I shook my head. "It would take the same amount of energy to transport us six blocks as it would to go to another time and place altogether. It would leave us too vulnerable."

"Should we just find a place in this building to hide? Wait for the crowd to disperse?" asked Andrus.

"It would be easier to travel after nightfall," Gareth agreed. "And someone needs to tell me what the hell happened while I was out."

The crowd below was thinning, most of them filtering out and going back to their lives or spreading out to cover a wider area to keep searching. More rain clouds were gathering in the east.

Across the way was a large, shuttered window, partially open. From what I could see, there was no furniture inside. "What about that place?" I pointed. "Can you tell if anybody's in there?"

Andrus stared hard at it. "It seems empty. I'll jump over first. I don't think this brute could fit through without crashing through the wall or ruining the shutter."

"That was unnecessary," Gareth grumbled, crossing his arms over his chest.

Andrus smirked before leaping from the roof and gliding through the open gap in the shutters. He flung them both wide and gave us the all clear.

"Can you make it?" asked Gareth.

I gave him a grin. "Worry more about yourself, big guy."

He gave me an exaggerated frown. "Already teaming up to pick on me."

I grasped his chin and pulled him toward me for a kiss. "I'm glad you're all right." Gareth's hands tried to settle on my waist, but I shirked his grasp, poised myself on the edge of the roof, and leaped toward the window with a final taunt over my shoulder. "You're still a brute!"

I heard a quick bark of laughter as I sailed through the window into Andrus's arms. He set me down and backed up quickly as Gareth followed right after. He scooped me up in his arms with a growl, and I hooked my knees around his hips. "I'm going to have to teach you a lesson about taunting a wolf." His lips brushed the shell of my ear, and I shivered.

"I love to live dangerously." I wrapped my arms around his neck and kissed him before pulling away. "But you'll have to teach me later."

He sighed. "You're right." He set me down, putting some distance between us to remove the temptation. I leaned against the wall.

"Okay, then," I said. "What are we going to do now?"

CHAPTER TWO

Andrus

"I'm not sure how much you remember," I began, looking pointedly at Gareth, "since you were unconscious almost immediately."

Gareth flipped me a rude hand gesture. "Was it the Hounds, then?"

"Unfortunately," I said.

"Shit," he mumbled, running a hand through his hair. He plucked anxiously at the braids in his beard, the warrior rings rustling with a light clink of metal. "How did we get away this time?"

I looked at Meg. "Ask her."

She shrugged. "I bound them in strands of time. Slowed them down, gave us a chance to get away."

"You can do that?" asked Gareth.

Another shrug. "I wasn't sure I could until I tried. I figured we had nothing to lose."

Just thinking about how close that encounter was had my blood pressure up. A sharp stab in my foot as I stepped on a splinter made me realize I left my shoes behind in Norway. I stopped my pacing around the floor, crouching down and picking at it, but my nails were too short.

"First course of action needs to be finding proper clothing," said Meg, kneeling in front of me and examining my foot when she saw the trouble I was having. "That should help us blend in a bit better at least. And these clothes are nasty."

Meg called forth a single claw and used it to deftly remove the splinter. I smiled. "Thank you."

She sat next to me and leaned on my shoulder, the cheap wooden planks of the floor shifting and shuddering just from her light weight. "Where have you met the Hounds before?"

"It was a long time ago," I said. "I don't rightly remember what year—"

Gareth furnished the answer for me. "1036."

"Common Era?" asked Meg.

Whatever language skills we gained from her were able to put meaning to her question. Gareth must've done the same, because he shook his head. "Before the Common Era."

Meg nodded and I continued. "It was shortly after a battle. The Titans had come across a small faction of young Ætherim in the Balkans. The Slavic factions had been garnering a lot of attention for the wrong reasons."

"Largely by using humans for sport and food. Most of the factions did the same thing, no matter what region they settled in, but these ones took it to another level," said Gareth.

"How bad?" asked Meg, brow furrowed.

"Have you ever seen a curtain made of human intestines? Or a throne made from glistening white bone freshly torn from a corpse?" I hated the memories it brought to the surface. The fear on the faces of every human we came across. They'd been convinced when the Titans arrived that their lot in life was only going to get worse.

"Remi and I were accompanying Pallas, just to get a feel for the area and see if the rumors were true. We were crossing through a mountain village when the scent of gore hit us. It was the middle of winter, but when we came upon the town, the bodies were still fresh. Most had been opened, neck to naval with one vicious swipe, their guts spilling into the snow."

"The Ætherim?" asked Meg.

"That's what we initially thought, but no. There were sounds of fighting coming from farther away, toward the town center. When we got there, the Hounds were standing in the middle of a mountain of bodies. One of the townsfolk was still being held in the air, dangling off the female Hound's claws. The minute they saw us, they smiled. They said something about their job being done, and they disappeared."

"Later, we discovered that the steward of that town had been in a feud with the steward of a neighboring city. Somehow that man had conscripted the Hounds to destroy his enemy."

"And what did the Hounds ask for in return?" Meg asked.

Gareth shook his head. "I don't know. Nobody does. That neighboring village disappeared, buildings and all." Gareth turned to me. "Isn't that where you met Death?"

Meg's head snapped toward me. "Death? *The* Death?"

I nodded. "He showed up shortly after the Hounds had left. When the job is that big, the boss shows up personally to take care of it. A single reaper wouldn't be enough."

"And how did that go?" Meg was leaning in, eager for more of the story.

"It was brief, and he largely dealt with Pallas. He was angry that the Hounds had been allowed to continue unchecked, and Pallas couldn't offer him a solution."

"Couldn't he just stop them himself?" asked Meg.

"I would've thought so too, but apparently the rules don't apply to them in the same way." I sought for the right words to describe it, but there were none. I settled for, "They're not from around here. Life and death work far differently for them."

She shivered as a chill ran through her. "How is that possible?"

"Nobody knows where they came from, or much of anything about them. Other than they're powerful and deadly, and always willing to work for a price. Unfortunately, most people never anticipate how high the price is until it's too late."

Gareth scoffed. "Most don't even know they exist, although they're better off for it. Wish I could say the same."

"And now they're after us." Meg sighed. "Did either of you have any idea what this job would entail when you signed up for it? Every obstacle we've come across has been substantial but now we have true, absolute monsters chasing us. How are we supposed to continue like this?" Her anxiety rose further with every sentence, and I wrapped my arm around her.

"There's no way we can beat them in a fight. Maybe my abilities are getting stronger and that's why I could hold them off. But it could also have been just one giant fluke and the next time we come across them I can't do the same thing and we're toast. What did Bel even offer them for this?"

She leaned her head against me. To say that the emotions coming off her were tumultuous would be an understatement.

"I don't know," I soothed, "but whatever it was must've been substantial. Money means nothing to them. They operate on promises and favors."

"I don't suppose we could make them a better offer?" asked Meg.

"We could try, but I don't think it would do us any good."

Gareth had been silent, staring off into space. "Do you think they wanted to kill us?" he asked quietly, once again stroking his beard.

"What else could they be trying to do?" I asked.

"If they wanted to kill me, I'd be dead. There was nothing stopping them back at the cabin. They dealt enough damage to injure me severely, but not kill me? Why? I can't imagine it was because they missed."

"They put a block on your ability to wake up," said Meg. "Maybe they were planning on incapacitating us and taking us somewhere. Clearly, they have no trouble traveling through time. It's the most logical choice from Bel's point of view. He can't come after us himself without running into a whole gamut of complications, so he has them track us down and bring us all to him." Her eyes went distant as she remembered what she'd suffered at his hands. "Where he can then do whatever the fuck he wants."

Meg's hands were shaking, and I took them in my own. Gareth and I shared a look, our anger flaring and both wanting desperately to protect our mate, but the damage was already done. When we caught up with Belsioch on our own terms, we would tear him apart. But we'd never be able to erase the memory of what she dealt with when she was under his power, completely at the mercy of a merciless man.

Gareth and I turned to casual small talk to take her mind off the past. Meg sat up like she'd remembered something and turned to me. "Can you fly?"

I was so taken aback by the change in subject that I just blinked at her. "I'm not sure I understand?"

"I'm trying to remember all the legends I've heard about the Nosmortem. Were they ever able to fly or defy gravity? Levitate?"

"I think you should probably explain why you're asking the question, and it might be easier for me to answer. Levitation is one of the skill sets that some Nosmortem had, but it certainly wasn't universal. I know I can't do it."

"When I fell off the roof, I was preparing to hit the ground, but it felt like I caught a drag line that slowed me down. And then I just stopped, kind of hovering in midair. But the second I thought about how weird it was, the magick broke, and, boom." She smacked her hands together.

"Could you have been slowing time down again? Without being conscious of it?" asked Gareth.

Meg bit her lip. "It takes a lot of concentration to do that. Maybe Kronos was interceding somehow?"

"Or Hyperion," suggested Gareth.

She shook her head. "But the fall wouldn't have killed me. It would've hurt, but I could walk it off. Why would they waste their power with that?"

I frowned. "There's so much you don't know about your own magick, and we're still figuring out how our bonding affects each other. We just need a bit of a breather to figure it all out."

Meg laughed bitterly. "And we're certainly not getting that anytime soon."

I didn't have any sage words of advice or comfort that would ring true. This was a bad situation all around, and I wasn't sure how to fix it. For once, my analytical mind was falling far short of helpful.

Gareth slid down the wall and sat. "Once this is over, just you wait. We'll all have so much time together, we'll be sick of each other in a week."

"Or at least be sick of Hadi. He's got that typical dragon ego. I believe you would call him 'extra,'" I said, using another modern term that struck me as poetic.

This drew a genuine laugh from Meg. "I see you're getting used to accessing the big language database in the sky?"

I nodded. "I'm not sure I entirely understand the etymology of where some of these words come from—"

"Nor should you try. It will never make sense," she said.

"Good to know." I kissed the top of her head. "Now, what's the plan once we get to the cathedral?"

"With any luck, our quarry will be there, and we can grab him and go," she said simply. "But sometimes if there's a massive landmark, I'm drawn to that just because it's the most prominent thing. It doesn't necessarily mean that he'll be there."

"And if he's not?" asked Gareth.

"Then I dig down deep and hope I can track him. But much like with Andrus, a large city with a dense population makes for a whole lot of distraction and interference. Should we make contingencies? If the Hounds show up again?" she asked.

I looked at Gareth and he gave an almost imperceptible shake of his head. "I'm afraid there wouldn't be much point. Our best bet is to keep ahead of them. Fighting is our last resort. If it comes to that, planning would be useless."

The grim reality of our circumstances set in. I tried to think of something else reassuring to say but had nothing. "Do you know specifically which of the Six we're here for? Do you get names at all?"

Meg shook her head. "It's mostly the signature that I look for. Sometimes I get their physical characteristics, but only if I look in a more extended trance state." She looked at Gareth. "Or if they reverse the connection and track me down instead."

My eyebrows shot up. "You didn't mention that."

"It was when I was first looking for all of you. I made that initial connection—"

Her eyes dropped, and she twisted her hands. I knew she was avoiding mentioning Arthur.

"But I'd already left that place in-between time and thought I was done with it. I was lying in bed trying to go to sleep when Gareth elbowed his way into my head."

"Found her in bed with another man," he growled. "Couldn't see it was Bel, which I'm thankful for. That would've been torture."

"Believe me, I felt your displeasure." Her lips quirked in a sardonic frown. Patting his knee, she said, "It did *not* help with my first impression of you."

"I'll make no apologies for being possessive of what's mine to protect," Gareth grumbled.

Meg moved over and sat in his lap, and he wrapped his arms around her. Her whole body relaxed as she sank back into him. "I wouldn't ask you to. I know where your heart's at."

"How did you even become aware that she tracked you?" I asked.

Gareth just shrugged and rested his chin on her head. I had a feeling once Hadi was back in our group, there would be tension between the dragon and the wolf.

Meg spoke. "I think Gareth has a bit more of a natural relationship with time than he's aware of. It certainly seemed to take a liking to him."

A soft glow of pleasure at her recognition came through the bond from Gareth. I wondered if I would develop something similar, or if, like the quickness with which I was picking up the language lexicon, all of us would have different specialties from our bonding with her.

"This is all so startlingly different," I mumbled. "Everything is happening so fast and it's all we can do not to get swept away. You spend two-thousand years preparing for something and then when it finally comes, you realize you aren't prepared at all."

Gareth nodded. "Agreed. The sooner all of us are together the better. It'll be far easier to keep our heads above water."

Meg shuddered at the reference and Gareth frowned. "Sorry. Should probably avoid all references to water and drowning for a while. I can't even imagine what that must've been like."

Her fingers were trailing absentmindedly up and down his thigh. "It was horrifying, but at least it proved something to us."

"What's that?" I asked.

"Even if it feels like it, we're not entirely alone in this. The Titans will do what they can to help us. If they can."

All three of us fell silent as we let that sink in. It was a comforting thought, given all the tight spots we had already found ourselves in and which would continue as this journey went on. But I had a feeling that we would need far more Hail Marys than the Titans could give.

Chapter Three

Meg

We waited until it was full dark before we set out for the cathedral. Creeping through the back alleyways, the sounds of the city were muted but still haunting. Fighting, the occasional wail, drunken laughter, all bouncing off the uneven walls and leaning supports that shored up the shoddier construction.

Eyes gleamed in the darkness through the shadows, which were falling thicker as the night went on. The most desperate and destitute huddled, trying to hide, looking for any security they could get.

Andrus and Gareth stuck close by my side. We passed laundry hanging on a line, so we took the opportunity to blend in a bit better. Andrus had to climb another balcony to get to it and scored some boots for him and Gareth as well, along with a pair of slippers for me. Their pants barely reached their knees and some creative seam-letting had to be done, but the boots helped cover the difference.

He'd liberated a coin purse from a burly man that had attempted to stick a knife in the vampire's ribs almost immediately after we left our hideout, so we were able to leave money behind in exchange for the wardrobe.

Andrus had also taken the opportunity to feed and while I was watching him, I salivated and felt my new teeth extend, but not fully. The hunger passed almost as soon as it started.

A hacking cough startled me as a man lurched from a doorway I hadn't seen. He was clearly drunk and staggering, and when his eyes fixed on me, it took a considerable amount of time for him to realize what he was looking at. When he finally figured it out, a hideous grin spread across his face, reminding me of the sorcerer back in Athens.

My wolf's claws extended from my fingertips preparing for a fight, but it never came. He looked at the two men on either side of me and hurried on. Apparently, he wasn't that drunk that his self-preservation didn't kick in.

"I'm still trying to wrap my head around this place," said Gareth, staring around him with a mixture of fascination and disgust.

"Hold on," said Andrus. We stopped and listened, straining our eyes in the darkness. I'd been noticing a gradual increase in my sensitivities since I bonded with Andrus and gained his vampirism. I'm sure more would continue to show themselves as I learned my way around these abilities. My night vision was better than ever, and, even though right now I was seriously regretting it, my sense of smell was also more enhanced than it had been with just my wolf.

There was nothing out of the ordinary that I could tell. "Did you see something?"

Andrus looked confused. "I thought—I don't know. It felt like we were being watched."

"We may have been," said Gareth. "Everything's overwhelming my senses so much it's been difficult to pinpoint anything."

"Are you good with continuing on?" I asked. They both nodded, but I could feel the unease through our bond, which only made my own paranoia grow. I was listening intently, but since I could hear every mouse squeak and muffled conversations from a block away, it was only making me jumpier.

We were two blocks away from the cathedral, and I could feel the heavy thrum of magick. The Seine already provided a steady source of energy coursing through the city. Combine that with the history in this place, the central role it played for over a millennium as a hub of civilization... it all added up to a *lot* of power.

"There. Do you feel that?" Andrus asked.

Gareth rolled his shoulders and nodded. "Yes. And it doesn't seem like the average person walking by either."

I blanched. "I think it's coming from ahead of us. More specifically," I hesitated. "The cathedral itself."

"That doesn't sound good," said Gareth. "But you're not picking up a signature anywhere?"

"No."

There was a force centered on that cathedral that was different. At best, that landmark was acting as a focus, concentrating all the magick in this place at a location where people regularly gathered for worship to their higher power. At worst, it was housing an entity that had glutted itself on energy steeped in upheaval, celebration, grief, fear, and constant change.

Only once or twice had I come across something in my searching that threw me for a loop, and this was another.

When the cathedral walls came into view, we found a place to hunker down and observe the building. There was an oppressive weight in the air, and my men pressed close on either side, wound tight like springs and ready for trouble. Something must've happened here between me seeing it now, and when I visited it in the 20th century, because there had been nothing remotely close to this when I was here before.

This energy felt... wrong. I couldn't even figure out what type of magick it was. If it belonged to a sorcerer, a magus, fae, Æhtherim, or *other*. There was nothing familiar to latch on to.

I took both their hands, giving in to the foreboding radiating off the cathedral. "Maybe we should find a place to bed down for the night, come back in daylight. When there are more people present, maybe it won't feel quite so oppressive."

"Won't that make it harder for your magick to work?" asked Gareth.

"Yes. But on the bright side, it's not that big a place. If he's actually there, we should see him. This time our basic senses should be enough to get by with." My thumbs stroked the backs of their hands. I could tell they were just as eager, if not more so, to find him as I was. "And if he's not there, we start looking elsewhere."

The rest of our night hadn't been comfortable, but it had been relatively safe. We found an underground tunnel, one of many in the rat's nest that ran underneath the city. It was cold and clammy, but it was defensible. Andrus and Gareth took turns keeping watch, refusing to let me sacrifice sleep. I kept waking up anyway, keeping whoever else was awake company until I drifted off again.

The three of us were becoming a more solid unit with every passing day. Even if you know how bonds work, until you're in one, it's almost impossible to grasp the full depth. The closeness that you feel. The certainty that you have, knowing that there are two other people in your life who will move heaven and earth to support you. Go to the ends of the Earth to keep you safe. And I knew without question that they loved me.

And they knew without question that I felt the same. Love at first sight was something that I'd always scoffed at. It always seemed too good to be true. I may live in a world of magick, but fairy tales don't exist. And I mostly still believe that to be true. What I do believe in is fate.

Sometimes there's a path that you are so destined to follow, nothing will keep you from it. I used to think that meant that I had no free will. That everything I ever did, or ever tried to do, was predestined. What did it matter what I wanted from life? What I needed from life?

But those two helped me see I do still have control. I can walk away any time. Granted, I'd have to run for the rest of my days. Bel would always hunt me and plenty of other goons would be sent after me, but that was just the lot I was cast. We all have our own burdens to bear from birth that follow us for our entire lives. The only thing that matters is how you take control. There may be an ultimate drive toward an ultimate goal, but how you get there is anybody's guess.

No, not a guess. It's your choice. And what happens after is your choice. You can either give in, and be pushed around like a puppet, or you can take control of your own destiny, and forge your own future.

These men were part of that. The rest of the Desma were as well, and I looked forward to them joining our family. I must've drifted off again, because next thing I knew, Andrus was shaking me awake. "It's time to go."

I nodded and sat up. "What time is it?"

"Getting near noon."

"What? Why'd you let me sleep that long?" I asked, grabbing Gareth's proffered hand and standing.

Andrus smiled. "We've been keeping an eye on the crowds. It's the most people we've seen there all day. And it didn't hurt anything to let you get some more sleep." He kissed the top of my head. "You're the one doing all the heavy lifting. You can let us do the grunt work."

My stomach growled, and a mince pie appeared in front of me. I eyed it suspiciously. "Where'd you get this?"

Andrus looked at me askance. "I survived for years by thieving. Pretty sure I can steal a pie without getting caught. From the looks of things, that vendor was a dick anyway. Don't feel too bad about it."

I gobbled it down. Dick or not, he made a good pie. Belly full, I followed the two out onto the street.

The day was bright, and the people were happy. Children chased each other around the square. I hoped the narcs from yesterday weren't here somewhere. Or maybe Andrus had frightened them enough that they wouldn't dare try it again.

Even though our clothing was less conspicuous, the three of us still stood out. Not for the first time, I wished that I had some kind of glamour magick. I'd have to ask my mates if any of the other Desma had that ability. But heavens forbid that something made our task easier for once.

We walked across the plaza toward the cathedral. This day, the double doors were flung open. It must be a Sunday. The pews inside were filling up, the soft whispers of the parishioners carrying up toward the vaulted ceilings, amplifying the sound tenfold. I could hear conversations from all the way to the front of the church.

Even in its earliest stages, this cathedral was breathtaking. There was evidence of the ongoing construction that would be continuing for hundreds of years from now, but there were still plenty of stained-glass windows, fine filigree work, gorgeous masonry, and wood tooling to stare at.

My mates had much the same reaction. They'd seen some impressive temples in their day, but nothing of this magnitude.

"Incredible," said Gareth.

Our stares were drawing stares. Or maybe it was the two men that stood head and shoulders taller than the tallest villager here.

There was movement at the altar. A man in a black cassock with a drawn face and sallow, sunken eyes stepped toward the pulpit. He scanned the crowd, a crooked smile revealing chipped teeth, as his eyes roved over his parishioners, scanning past familiar faces, sometimes with a nod or small smile. Row by row he continued methodically, and I motioned for Gareth and Andrus to follow me through a small door that was marked as private. I couldn't shake the feeling that we were being hunted by that gaze.

The door closed behind us, and we found ourselves in a small walled-in courtyard with a fountain, open sky above us. I could hear the priest's voice even outside when he began his sermon, rumbling and gravelly, the entire building designed to amplify sound. It echoed through the cathedral and amplified the rougher aspects of his voice until it sounded like a hoarse, croaking murmur that set my teeth on edge.

"He made you uneasy, too?" Andrus asked.

"Yeah. Let's just keep looking around out here," I said, spotting a narrow set of wooden stairs and scaffolding that led upward. "We can stick to the outside. There won't be anyone working on a Sunday."

The sermon continued its echoing boom, becoming louder the higher we went. It was the fire-and-brimstone type, and I shuddered. It was the same zealous conviction that my caretakers had had, and had punished me severely for challenging.

We were almost at the level of the tops of the buttresses. The air was clear and fresh, and my senses weren't so muddied by the masses of people. And then—

"There it is," I whispered. I stopped and turned, too fast. The stairs were so narrow that I'd misplaced my footing and would've slipped off the side if not for Andrus's outstretched arm.

Heart in my throat, I pushed into the stone wall to wait for my pulse to return to normal. "Thank you for that."

Andrus inclined his head. "What got you so excited?"

"I can feel him. His signature is all over this place."

My mates grinned, relieved. There was a vantage point from up here where we could look down on the entire congregation. Andrus and Gareth scanned the crowd below.

"Can you see him?" It was quite a distance, but both of them had sharp vision and should at least be able to pick out someone who looked remotely similar.

They took a moment. "No," said Andrus.

Gareth cursed under his breath. "I can't either."

"What the hell?" I asked. "I can *feel* him. Everything is telling me he's here."

Andrus looked at me helplessly. "There are plenty of other places that we can't see from here. Or maybe he could be below. They probably have cellars and the like."

An inexplicable punch of dread accompanied those words. I shook my head as Gareth moved closer, sensing my fear. "I wouldn't go down there unless we had no other choice. That creepy feeling, that sense of being watched. I think it all stems from there."

"How do you know?" asked Gareth.

"You don't feel it? The minute Andrus mentioned it, it was like some warning bell went off. My flight response kicked in hard."

Andrus was the first to ask the question out loud. "You don't think they're keeping him down there against his will, do you? And that sense of dread is just to keep people away?"

I sighed, ashamed to admit that I didn't want to find out; it scared me that much. But if they couldn't feel it, maybe they weren't as susceptible to whatever magick it was.

Gareth gripped my elbow. "Why don't Andrus and I check it out? You can stay up here. We'll just take a quick peek around."

I started to protest, but I knew that it had to be done. "We shouldn't separate. I'll go with you."

Andrus shook his head. "We can still communicate through the bond. The two of us have done plenty of reconnaissance, it will only take a minute."

I was relieved to not have to accompany them, but I still felt guilty. "Okay. Thank you."

They nodded, and each gave me a quick kiss before they headed back down the stairs. After a scan of the courtyard showed no entry point to get underground, they hopped the walls and began searching, making their way around the building. They were out of sight when I felt a flash of victory, and then they seemed to get farther away from me. They'd found a way in.

I could still feel them, so that gave me some comfort. The priest's sermon was wrapping up, and he became more conversational. I listened in, looking for something to take my mind off my mates heading toward what felt like horrible danger.

"So here we come at last to the end of our service. I hope you take away enlightening lessons and go forth on your path of righteousness."

The crowd murmured a response in unison.

"Before I release you today, I wanted to ask for your continued prayers for Marquis Remi Allard. Our benefactor is continuing to struggle with his illness. I fear it may claim his life and we will not see our brother again in this lifetime."

At the mention of the name, I gasped. Andrus had mentioned it before. Could that be him? If he gave a lot of money to this project, he must've spent a good amount of time here to oversee his investment. That could explain why his signature was so strong.

The congregation didn't take long to exit the church at the end of the service. He was speaking to a handful of people when another man approached. He leaned in to whisper in the priest's ear, but the priest tried to shrug him off. There was an exchange that I couldn't hear, and then both headed to the door that let out to the courtyard below.

As soon as I realized where they were heading, I concealed myself. Chances were small that they'd look up here, but better safe than sorry.

Once the door had snicked closed, the new arrival confronted the priest. "You told me you'd find me new entertainment."

"Baron Duval, I'm always happy to speak with you, but I really have other matters I need to attend."

"I have a party in three days. Find me new Stranger blood."

"It's not my responsibility to furnish participants for your games."

"I'm sorry. Did your extra-curricular activities suddenly stop costing you money? Did your gambling debts disappear? Because if you no longer need my donations, that's fine by me."

"Your generosity to our congregation is greatly appreciated," said the priest after a long pause. "I'll see what I can do."

"Find me a beastie, Montrose, or I'll let the debt collectors have you." The baron turned on his heel and swept away through the door, leaving the priest seething.

From all the way up here, I could see Father Montrose's face pucker like he'd just bit a lemon.

Not sure what that was about, but something told me to keep it in the back of my mind.

Chapter Four

Gareth

Andrus and I were around the far side of the cathedral and had yet to find an ingress, so we began furtively looking through windows. Andrus whistled and beckoned me over when he found a newer build of what looked like a scribe's quarters. A shutter was standing partially open on the next window.

We climbed through, landing in the small but airy room that smelled of ink and vellum. Heavy leather-bound books lined the north wall and there was a work in progress on the table.

By sight, sound, or smell, there was no one around this section of the building, so we made our way through the halls, checking the other anterooms and finally landing on a cellar. The cold, dank room reeked of spilled wine and mold, but underneath was the hint of something else.

"Ozone," said Andrus.

"Ozone?" Every time I heard a word I wasn't familiar with, it took less and less time to figure out what it meant. "Ah. From what?"

Andrus spotted something and crossed to the far corner, grabbing an iron ring and pulling. A trap door screeched through the quiet and I flinched. "Now we need to make this double quick. Someone might've heard that."

He only looked a wee bit apologetic as he descended the steep stairs that disappeared into darkness. The smell was overwhelming and with it now came the rank rot of old blood.

"There it is again," I said.

Andrus paused. "Like we're being watched. What is it?"

I hummed, having no idea. My wolf was just near the surface, ready to act if a threat arose, but there were still no signs of life other than the congregants above us.

I could barely see Andrus a few paces in front of me, so complete was the dark. Shortly after our feet found flat ground, the stone gave way to packed earth, with gave way to—

"Grass? What the hell?" I heard more than saw Andrus lean down and run his hands through thick blades of grass.

"But no light reaches this place. How is that possible?"

All around the perimeter of the room, the darkness seemed even more complete. A menace emanated from it and if I peered closely, I knew I'd see the watchers staring back. I took tentative steps forward, the fear screaming at me to turn around, go back.

The only sound was the soft shush of the grass under my feet until I crashed into something hard and cold. The smell of blood was much stronger over here. Running my hands along the straight edges, I determined it was a table made of stone. My fingers ran through cold, congealed liquid and I yanked my hand back, hurrying back to the subtle glow of light and the stairs that would take us out of here.

"I don't think there's anyone down here, do you?" Andrus asked, unease in his voice.

"No. Something is going on here, but I don't think they're keeping prisoners." In the dim light, I confirmed the blood that stained my hand.

He nodded. "Let's go."

I headed for the stairs, but stopped when I heard the faintest scuffling noise somewhere in the vast darkness.

Andrus had noticed, too.

We stood and listened for what felt like an eternity before we dared to move. The sound didn't come again and there was still no sign of life. I hurried toward the stairs, Andrus right behind me, and I didn't relax until we were back in the cellar with the trapdoor closed behind us.

We shared a look and made our way back to Meg.

She was waiting for us excitedly and quickly told us what she'd heard. It was a relief to know a name, but the strangeness of the circumstances was weighing on me. "I think it's safe to assume Remi isn't here. I'm curious about what's going on here, but I don't think we're going to learn anything else useful to our search."

The three of us had snuck back through the side door. The cathedral was almost empty, just the faint murmur of voices coming from somewhere out of sight. We were halfway to the doors when a small zing of alarm went through me, and I realized it came from Andrus. Meg and I turned to follow his gaze.

The priest was standing at the altar, joined by several more figures. They looked human, but they very clearly were not. Each was staring directly at the three of us, but they made no move.

I put my hand at the small of Meg's back and guided her out the doors, Andrus right behind. Their stares bore into us, and a trickle of foreboding flowed through the bond.

We didn't slow our pace until we reached the entrance of our tunnel hideout.

"Wait," said Meg, stopping in her tracks.

I looked around to see if I could tell what had her on edge, but there was nothing. She shook her head. "It's not an immediate threat, but I think we should go somewhere else. Wander around until we don't feel their eyes on us anymore. Maybe they're using some kind of tracking magick."

"It certainly couldn't hurt, as long as we stay off the main roads. We still catch far too many eyes around here," said Andrus.

"Maybe you should put a bag over your head," I joked, elbowing Andrus and trying to lighten our anxiety. "They're staring at your ugly mug."

Meg rolled her eyes, but laughed anyway and took our hands.

Tensions may have been building between us, mostly as I worked through my own issues of possessiveness, but I had never felt more tied to two people in my entire life. More in sync. Disagreements were bound to arise, of course, but that would never sully the bond.

Spending so many hundreds of years without a pack to call my own, and now I had the beginnings of a true family.

"Where should we start looking for a new place to hide?" asked Meg.

Andrus must've already been thinking about that, because he had an answer ready to go.

"Plague houses. We need to find a place of sickness. People will be too nervous to come near it, unless they're desperate, so that will keep the humans out. And if we pick a spot with a good view, we can see anyone else coming a mile away."

I nodded. "That works."

After a search that took most of the afternoon into the evening, we found an empty block of rooms, the only people still living there also sick. Most of the upper floor had already been emptied, scattered ash behind the building the only remnants of the furniture.

Andrus had gone on one of his "expeditions" and stole some food and bedding for us. He was a great thief, and I got no sense that he was lying when he said that once again he had targeted a less than honorable merchant.

"A vampiric Robin Hood," Meg had called him. The lexicon may have helped us understand the general meaning, but it wasn't much good at going beyond that, so Meg told us some stories to pass the hours by.

We were settling into a quiet night, and Andrus had already dozed off. I'd been staring ahead at nothing in particular when Meg touched my arm.

"You know you can always ask me anything, right?"

I blinked and turned toward her. "Yes. But I didn't want to pile onto a plate already full."

"It's not a problem. Please."

There were so many things I wanted to ask, but I reached for the most pressing questions first. Andrus sensed the change of atmosphere and was wide awake.

"How do you know where to look?" I asked.

Meg had been lounging on her side in a scatter of blankets, head propped on her fist. But now she sat and tucked her legs under her, preparing for a deeper conversation.

I explained further. "As far as the points in time that you choose to find people. You could come looking for us anywhere in our timelines. Is there anything specific that draws you to a certain year? Or is it something about us, like our frame of mind?"

"I'm also curious about that," said Andrus.

"A heavy-hitting question," said Meg. "I'm not sure I have a good answer for you."

"Do you at least have a theory?" I asked.

She thought. "To me it's always like I'm stepping into the time that's most... present? If that makes sense. When somebody purposefully moves through time and stays put in a past that wasn't theirs, it leaves a mark. It's nothing that I can really see or describe. It's just a feeling. And then I track your lives from the point where the Titans sent you and follow it up to the current year. You all were thrown so far back that there's a gap between the lives you're living here, right now and where your old ones left off, kind of an empty space where it's just a swirling bundle of potential."

Meg sighed and shook her head, a sardonic grin on her face. "Is this making any kind of sense at all? I really don't feel like I'm doing it justice. It's always been something so innate within me and I never had anyone that could relate, so to describe it to somebody else is a tall order."

"Some of it is making sense," I assured her.

"Alright, here's another question for you," said Andrus. "If I had gone back to my hometown in the year that I was born, would I have come across my family? My infant self?"

Meg grimaced. "Oof. Another tough one. Not really a good answer for it, either. Sometimes—when massive upsets occur like planting someone in a different timeline—a new branch will develop to allow for paradoxes. It's your own timeline running close alongside the main one and if it looks like there's going to be an issue, Time will take action and alter your path. Other times, nothing happens.

"Free will makes the direct repetition of timelines un-likely. You may have found one or both of your parents or any other family living there, but the dynamic would most certainly be different."

She laughed and leaned forward, her face glowing with excitement. "But here's where it gets really interesting."

Andrus and I exchanged a glance. Seeing her this happy was a balm for our frazzled nerves.

"Are you ready to talk about souls?" She didn't wait for an answer. "So when a person is incarnated, they receive their body, go about their life, and eventually they return in some form or other to that big cosmic waiting room in the sky. But since you never died," she said, pointing at Andrus, "there was no soul to reincarnate into an infant version of yourself. So even if your parents ended up together again, you would not have been the result of that union. So that's one paradox easily avoided."

Andrus nodded, a small smile working its way to his face. "That makes sense. More so than trying to wrap my head around time anyway."

I shook my head slowly, the wheels turning. "I think I'm starting to understand as well." Derisive laughter huffed out as I ran a hand through my beard. "But what I'm coming to realize is that the more I understand, the more questions I have."

She nodded, a knowing smile creeping across her face. "Just keep this in mind. Nothing is true, and anything is possible, especially when it concerns time. You can't force order on a nonlinear, sentient thing. Time does what it wants. We'll never pin it down, all we can do is work with it. I've heard people attribute their gut instinct to tapping into higher consciousness or guardians. And maybe that's true. But in our case—" She looked at me. "—I think that Time has a lot to do with it. Guiding us along because we're open to it."

That sounded similar to what I'd been experiencing of late. "That tiny voice in the back of your head? Barely more than a shadow of a thought and whatever it says or suggests always seems like the best course of action?"

Meg smiled. "Exactly like that. Time is a living, breathing thing, independent even of Kronos. I had my suspicions before, but it seems clear now. It's accepted you into the fold."

I was gobsmacked.

She turned to Andrus. "Have you noticed anything like this for yourself?"

He looked hesitant to answer. "I'm not really sure. Some of what you're saying is ringing a bell, but I seem to have a much easier time with language."

She scooted over to him and rested her head on his shoulder. "All the better. We're going to be unstoppable with the insane variety of talents we'll all have. They won't know what hit them."

Andrus pulled her to him for a kiss and a flash of jealousy escaped me before I could think twice. They both glanced at me apologetically as they felt it, but I waved them off. "I'm sorry. It's got nothing to do with you," I said to Andrus. "I'm fighting my nature a bit here."

I moved toward the window and looked out over the quiet street below. Other than the occasional late-night tavern-goer or skulking thief, there wasn't a lot going on. Andrus and Meg were talking quietly.

Idiot, I scolded myself. I needed to deal with these instincts. There was no way I was jeopardizing this family because I couldn't share our mate's attention.

"I'm going to walk the perimeter, give you two some time alone," I said, heading to the door before they could respond.

And also to have a chat with myself.

The street was much the same as I'd seen from the window. A cat yowled in the distance, and a few dogs barked in response. Then everything fell silent. The distant rushing of the river was ever present in the background, but it did little to alleviate the emptiness.

Overlying everything was a caution, a breath being held, while people waited helplessly to see what fate had in store for them. Or perhaps fate had no place here. Perhaps they were all beholden to whatever magick was present in this place.

Fate. Meg was my fate, freeing the Titans was my fate. All of us would be brought together as a force to be reckoned with. We would be stronger that way, and I knew that. But my wolf wanted our mate all to himself and he wasn't hearing it when I told him to back off. He wasn't a lone wolf anymore, and this was part of it. There were still plenty of things that Meg and I shared between just the two of us.

My ability to pick up language had stalled somewhat. I could understand basics, but anything more complex and I would get lost, unable to draw as easily as Andrus on the ability. She and Andrus could hold an entire conversation in the native language of a place without even thinking about it until I reminded them I couldn't follow.

But we shared that connection to Time. We were the first to bond. To know her was to love her, and it would be ludicrous to think the others wouldn't feel the same. Andrus clearly did, but Meg didn't play favorites. It was a natural thing for her to include us both, effortless to ensure nobody felt unwanted.

I was passing through an unlit block of buildings. I could hear people snoring as I passed by shuttered windows bolted against the night. A few times, a brave soul would attempt to approach me, but quickly lost their nerve. It wasn't long before I started to see more signs of life and moved toward it out of sheer curiosity.

A garrison sat on this side of the city, its imposing walls lit with fires as soldiers patrolled along them. Occasionally, calls would go out and spread down the watch from one soldier to the next. Normally, I would've just kept walking, but something about this place drew me to it. I flashed on my conversation with Meg, the instinct that drove us to do things even if we didn't realize why in the moment.

I kept to the shadows, staying well out of sight, and watched. It must've been at least an hour, and I'd given up hope that there was anything interesting to see here, when there was a sudden flurry of movement. A horse and rider were approaching, and a new round of calls went up as the guards ordered the gate opened. Heavy saddle bags were draped over the horse's rear end, clinking and rattling with all manner of goods. But this wasn't just a delivery of supplies or a merchant making a stop, trying for a quick sale. The guards kept their distance from this person, eyeing him warily from their positions.

As soon as the rider was within the walls, the gates closed. I felt an urge to rush forward and scanned for the safest way to do so. I would be exposed over open ground, but there was a heavy patch of shadows beneath an overhang jutting from the wall. Most of the guards had turned their attention to the new arrival, and I bolted forward.

I flattened myself against the stone and waited for any sign that they'd seen me, but all remained quiet. I strained my hearing to the edge of my abilities and could just make out the conversation between the rider and someone who spoke with authority. I guessed the garrison master.

"Pretty late in the evening to be stopping by without an announcement," he groused.

"When I'm struck with an idea, I don't care to let it wait until morning. You know how important this work is. Should I explain to the king how things were delayed because you needed ample time and notice of my arrival, which only requires you to open a few doors?" The rider's voice dripped with condescension. There was no love lost between these two.

The garrison master grunted. "What is it this time, then?"

"I'd noticed yesterday that that devil's wings had started to grow back again. It requires further examination."

My stomach dropped. Wings? Could they be talking about—

The garrison master laughed. "I'll bet he rues the day he ever said foot in this city. *Marquis Allard*," mocked the man, and my heart stopped. "The Devil in disguise."

I didn't wait to hear anything further from their conversation. After checking that the coast was clear, I sprinted back to the side street and kept running.

CHAPTER FIVE

Bel

"So what do you have for me, Risha?"

I'd removed the two of us to the kitchen and closed the swinging door behind us to give us a modicum of privacy. I trusted the other nephilim as far as their loyalty, but if Risha had been holding something back, it must be good. All I needed was for one of them to go shooting their mouth off at the worst possible moment for my plans to be spoiled.

"My lord," she began, twitchy, still fingering the talisman around her neck. "I'd like to make a request first."

She backed up a step as anger lit my eyes with a dangerous smolder. How dare she come in here and try to negotiate. But I am a reasonable god.

"What is it?" I asked, draping myself into one of the dining room chairs and leaning back casually.

"If I give you this, I'd like to request—" She paused, looking frightened and casting another sidelong look toward the living room where her twin would be lying on the couch.

I rolled my eyes. "Speak!"

Risha jumped out of her skin, inching back into the corner like a scared animal.

The words tumbled out of her mouth in a rush before she could second-guess herself. "I'd like to request that you let my brother leave."

I paused. That was unexpected. "Leave? Why would he want to do that?" A small hint of a smile played at my mouth, and I barely resisted chuckling. I flexed the hand still speckled with his blood; her eyes fixated on it.

"Let me take him back home. You can send somebody with me to make sure I return, but I *will* return. Just let me take him home." She took a deep, gasping breath. "I'm much more value to you if I can focus on the work, instead of my fear for him."

My face clouded over again, the anger bubbling back to the surface. She was just as bad as Ursal. Maybe it was a weakness in their family line, making them think that they had choices. Making them think they could defy me.

"I don't know," I said, picking at my fingernails. "It seems to be pretty good motivation for you, the thought that if you don't succeed at your work, I will kill him. You've clearly figured something out already, so where's my real incentive to let you send him away?"

She cringed and all the color drained from her face. Her breaths were coming out in shaky huffs and she closed her eyes, trying to build up courage. "I already had this developed, my lord..." Her mouth worked like a fish as she tried to figure out how to phrase her next sentence. "...before you chose to... punish... my brother."

Even as she said the word "punish" the barely concealed glare that she aimed at me said plainly all of the other words she could've chosen its place. And they would've been accurate. Ursal had raised my ire, but I must admit there was something *cathartic* about using him as a punching bag.

But then those other words needled back into my brain and my anger turned to outrage. "When were you planning on sharing this development? Were you going to betray me?" I spat, standing and stalking toward her as she pressed herself back into the corner like she wanted to sink through the other side.

"It was only ever for you, my lord. The first time you tried to travel through time physically, it drained you so much. I was trying to make it easier for you, to facilitate your mission. I never intended to keep it from you, there was just so much else going on, I—"

I shoved her into the wall and grabbed the object around her neck, yanking it free.

It was a key. Just a small brass skeleton key that seemed like it would fit any of the old fixtures in this lodge. "What does it do?"

"It forms a self-sustaining portal. All you have to do is say the activation words, and it'll act as a focus, drawing power from elsewhere, so you don't have to use your own. And it acts like a trail marker, so it'll hold down that place in time on both ends."

I took a step back, holding the key up to the light to study it. It was so unassuming. There were no markings on it other than the scratches worn from decades of use. I couldn't feel any inherent power coming off it. It seemed completely benign.

"What are the activation words?" I asked, only giving her partial attention.

"Any point in the storm," she said in a tiny voice.

I caressed the cool brass between my fingers. "Any point in the storm." The instant the words left my mouth, the key flared to life. It burned as bright as white phosphorus, but without producing any heat. I held it out from me as it seared into my eyes, and yet I had a hard time looking away. I watched in fascination, squinting against the glare, as the light expanded to the size of a window, then a door, then a double door.

The slick surface undulated, catching and twisting the light like a puddle of gasoline.

Risha's words broke through my entranced state. "Now you just have to tell it what year, and where. You can get as specific as you want."

"You've tested this?" I turned on her, suddenly suspicious. How had I not noticed this level of magick being used right under my nose?

She nodded. "Briefly, my lord. After Apollo had injured you, while you recovered. Only once."

A grin spread across my face. This was it. The solution to fulfilling my end of the bargain with the Hounds. "99th Olympiad, year 3, second cycle, Atarneus."

The gate flashed and turned into a silvered mirror. I stepped through. The light was blinding, and I squeezed my eyes shut. It felt like I was falling end over end as I hurtled through time and space. I hit the ground, landing on my hands and knees, a wave of nausea threatening to overturn my stomach. Once the world stopped spinning, I looked up.

Atarneus was one of the last battlegrounds where we'd faced the Titans, completing our victory and sealing them away in Tartarus. Subsequently, this city also became the staging ground for one of the months-long celebrations that took place in each of the three battleground cities. I'd had a habit of traveling to each, spending several weeks watching the increasing debauchery and drunkenness. I may have also encouraged questionable behavior, more for my fun than theirs. Humans and Strangers alike do shocking things if you give them some room and a reason to call off the rules.

So here I was now, surrounded by the noise, the laughter, the music and the press of bodies exhausted and worn from their bacchanalia.

I'd heard that this party had received a special guest after I'd left. Now all I had to do was find him. The city was still in ruins, a casualty. The odor of death hung about the place, most of the bodies still lying in the streets where they fell. After I'd started the celebrations, people became too inebriated to do anything but revel. The party had moved to the outskirts of the city, where a great temple still stood. I'd kept it protected. It was dedicated to me, after all.

The steps would give me a better vantage point to view the throngs of people. Hands grasped at my clothes, fingers tearing, pulling, trying to draw me back into the crowd. Cries of adoration and pleas for blessings went up. Women ran their hands over my body, grinning at me and inviting me to dark corners where they could entreat for personal favor.

I shook them all off, heading toward my throne, which stood empty in between polished pillars of stone. The mass of people was just too large. I'd never be able to pick out the guest of honor. And if the rumors I heard were true, he looked different to each person who saw him.

Raising my hands over my head, I bellowed over the crowd. "Hear me!"

The throngs shook off their drunken haze and diverted their attention from their other pursuits. Once they noticed my return, a cheer went up, glasses full of rich wine raised in salute. "Friends!" I continued. "You do me a great honor by being here. The Ætherim are pleased with your many offerings and praise. But there is one here among you whom I am eager to speak with."

There were murmurs among the crowd as people cast furtive glances at their neighbors.

"Death," I said. "Please come forward."

The whispers turned to shocked gasps. Everyone stood still, looking around with wary eyes, afraid that any of their fellows were Death himself.

My impatience was reaching its maximum when there was finally movement. A man stepped forward, and the crowd parted to let him through. Their sudden retreat made him pause. Each person he looked at pressed back farther into the throng. He smirked and continued on, reaching the stairs of my temple and staring up at me. He appraised me with a shrewd gaze before taking the first step.

I could hear each footfall on the marble, so quiet had it become. When he reached me, I drew him back into the heart of the temple and slowly, the revelers returned to their activities.

The man before me looked average, unremarkable. I couldn't say if he was familiar, but I'm terrible with faces. He was dressed like anyone off the street, tall and lanky, hardly any muscle. Built like an aristocrat but dressed like a commoner. There was a weight about him, something tangible, an aura. Even so, it was nothing that would raise eyebrows.

"Belsioch," he said, dipping his head in deference.

"Death. I've always wanted to meet you, but have never had the pleasure."

"I thought you were traveling. People weren't expecting you back for weeks."

"I was inspired to return."

"And what was that inspiration? Certainly it wouldn't be on my account." He smiled and appraised me. "And I might add that you are dressed rather interestingly. What is this fashion?"

I looked down at myself and realized I was wearing very modern clothing. The drunken idiots around us hadn't taken notice, but I would need to keep that in mind. Megiste had had more than a little trouble because of a simple clothing anachronism.

"Nothing you aren't familiar with," I said dismissively. Death was one of the few beings capable of traveling through time without restriction, much like Megiste. I knew he was fully aware of the time period I'd just come from.

"Why call me out? Is there something I can help you with?" asked Death.

"Just an introduction. I didn't want to be impolite."

Death's slyness was legendary, and this moment was no different. "I never thought you would align yourself with creatures such as the Hounds. What errand are they performing for you?"

"Who said anything about that?"

He smiled. "I can smell them on you. Those beasts mar anything they touch, always leaving their stench behind."

"What began this rivalry of yours?" I asked, with genuine curiosity. He wasn't afraid of them, it was disgust and hatred. "Don't they give you plenty of work to do?"

He sneered. "I'm not sure if you know this, but my job is very secure. I will never run out of work to do, and I don't need those monsters helping people along. Especially with the mess they usually leave. Deaths so sudden that the souls don't know they're deceased. I hate having to explain it."

"That can't be all. There are lots of serial killers throughout history. They would hardly be the first, nor will they be the last."

Death's smile was thin. "Is there something specific you wanted to see me about?"

I shook my head. "Like I said, I just wanted to introduce myself."

"Very well, then." He bowed slightly at the waist and turned to walk away. I threw my hand out, scratching my nail along his arm. Drawing blood.

Death whirled and stared at me, at the hand that I quickly withdrew. His eyes narrowed. "So it's like that, friend?"

"I have no idea what you're talking about," I replied, with an innocent smile. "There was a spider."

He huffed a laugh. "I expect a better lie from you."

I shrugged. "Those days are over. Now I find it much easier just to be myself."

He gave a sharp nod. "I suppose I'll be seeing you then."

I flashed my teeth. "You can count on it."

Death disappeared back into the crowd, and I took a seat on my throne. Petitioners brought plenty of food and drink, and I spent the rest of the evening indulging in revels. All the while the simple brass key around my neck glowed softly, never once showing any sign of running low on power.

When the dawn broke, I reluctantly returned to my current time, stepping into the kitchen only moments after I'd initially left. Risha was still huddled in the corner, face pressed into her knees. I crouched in front of her, lifting her head toward me with a gentle tilt of my fingers.

Her eyes widened in surprise, still puffy and red from her tears. "You've done well." I grinned and dangled the key. "I'm going to need a lot more of these."

CHAPTER SIX

Andrus

Meg and I were left staring after Gareth at the closed door. "Do you think he's alright?" asked Meg.

I nodded. "Whenever he needs to work things out, he always goes off by himself."

"Is everything okay between you two?" she asked, brow knit with worry. My face broke into a grin, the suddenness of it catching her off guard. "What?"

"Oh, don't misunderstand me," I began, taking her hands. "This is how our dynamic has always worked. Things are a bit tense right now, but we'll move past it. I hope *you* don't feel like you're caught between us."

She looked dubious. "Gareth said the same thing when I asked him if all of your personalities coming together would be a problem once I was in the middle. The tension has only been getting worse between you two." Her large, violet eyes were peering at me, trying to catch sime in a lie.

"Growing pains only," I assured her. "Gareth is probably having a talk with his wolf at this very moment."

Meg looked down at our hands twined together, then raised her eyes back to meet mine. "I haven't been making you feel left out, have I?" she asked, trailing her fingers along my arm.

"No, not at all."

Meg pulled a face, and I relented.

"Maybe a little. But the two of you bonded first. I get it."

"That still has to sting. Please know it's not intentional. This is throwing me for a loop. I spent most of my life in a miserable house, then partnered up with the first man that showed me kindness."

"A man we will kill together," I said through clenched teeth.

She ran her hand down my face. "And now here I am, with two wonderful men that I'm falling hard and fast over. After Bel..." She chewed her lip. "I didn't think I'd trust myself with anyone again. My feelings betrayed me, and he manipulated me like a puppet. And I thought I loved him."

I pulled her closer as her humiliation welled up, wishing I could convince her that it wasn't some weakness of hers that caused it. But she'd have to find her way to that conclusion on her own.

Gods, I hated that bastard. "He is an expert at getting what he wants from people, no matter how he has to do it. And he's had thousands of years of practice."

She wiped a tear away before it could fall and regained her composure. "But with the two of you—" She laughed through the strain in her voice. "—it's entirely different. Now I know that this is what love is supposed to be like." She paused. "I'd prefer if it came with much less danger and that every place the whole lot of you seem to settle wasn't under imminent threat from something or other—"

I frowned. "That does seem to be a common issue, doesn't it?"

"Why is that?" she asked. "Serious question. You're all drawn to places that are about to be besieged or annihilated or beset by some kind of unknown creature that's living in a subterranean lair. You didn't get enough of danger when you were with the Titans?"

I considered. "There is a certain amount of excitement required to keep our interests. That's why we chose to fight, to travel, to protect. We move on until we find it. But also, the places that are the most troubled need the most help. It's a way for us to be of service."

Meg squirmed around in my lap and placed her hands on either side of my face, peering closely into my eyes.

I smiled uncertainly. "What?"

"I'm studying what a good-hearted man looks like." She tilted her face toward me, and I wasted no time capturing her lips with my own.

Meg deepened the kiss, and her hands began to rove, my cock already rising to meet her invitations. I shifted us around and laid back, Meg straddling my hips and grinding as she worked at the laces on my breeches, before pulling my tunic over my head. She shimmied down toward my feet, pulling my trousers off before following suit with her own clothing.

She made to reposition over my cock, but I shook my head. "I need to taste you."

Meg complied, situating her knees on either side of my head before lowering to my mouth. My hands wrapped around her thighs as my tongue delved into her pussy, already soaked. I moaned at her sweet taste as I ran my tongue between her folds and over her clit.

She jerked her hips at the sensation and gasped. My tongue returned to her entrance and plunged deep, pulsing in and out as she rode my face. I refocused on her clit and she sped her pace, chasing her first release. I wanted to feel her clench. When she was a second away from climax, I slipped my tongue back inside her and she came, muscles spasming and gripping me tight.

I released my hold on her thighs, and she moved back down my body, massaging my balls in one hand while she took my entire cock down her throat without pause. I groaned and tried to stay still, watching her with hooded eyes as she bobbed, saliva glistening around my shaft before it disappeared into her mouth again. Gods, it was incredible. Her tongue teased me into a frenzy, and my hips bucked up.

She choked and I stopped, holding back, but our eyes met and hers smoldered with need. I drove upward again, deeper, Meg moaning around my cock, the vibrations singing through me and enticing me to pick up my speed.

I moved my hand to cradle the back of her head as I thrust deep into her throat. Her whimpers redoubled and I could feel the pressure building between her thighs even without direct touch. This bond had so many advantages. I was almost at my peak, and she released her hold on me, slipping her hand down to take herself across the finish line.

We came together and collapsed back on the floor in a sweaty heap, breathing hard. She fit perfectly at my side as she settled into the crook of my arm and buried her face in my neck. Silence fell and we dozed off. I was almost asleep when I felt a shift in her. She nuzzled my neck and my breath caught as she licked my throat, right before the sharp scrape of teeth ran down my jugular. I moaned, my own teeth elongating with a different hunger.

Meg leaned away, running her hands down my chest as she moved to straddle my hips. Her hair fell over us in a cascade and I smiled when I saw her beautiful face. Her violet eyes were rimmed with red around the irises and her fangs were fully bared. They were petite, barely longer than her incisors, but sharp as daggers. I reached up to stroke her cheek and she rested her head in my palm, a small trickle of blood running from her lip as her teeth cut into her, but she didn't even blanch. She just licked the blood away with a quick swipe of her tongue.

My cock was already rising again, and she helped it along with a few soft strokes before lining me up and sinking down. I dragged in a shuddering breath and raised my hands to rest on her hips. She rocked, slowly at first, her movements controlled. She stared down at me, and I could feel her attuning to this new need for blood.

"Is it safe?" she asked. "For vampires to drink from each other?"

I nodded, groaning as she rolled her hips in response. "Packs an extra punch."

She leaned forward, sliding against my chest. I moved one hand to her head and ran my fingers through her hair, gripping the base of her neck as she lowered her mouth to my throat. "You're okay?" she asked, nervous.

I hummed. "I can honestly say I've never been better, fated one."

The bond sang with contented happiness, and she kissed the crook of my shoulder. "Guide me."

The whisper of breath and graze of her lips on me elicited a growl. She ran her tongue across me again, and I stopped her when she reached the right point. "There. Just a small pressure is all it takes."

Meg had stopped riding me in her concentration and it took all my willpower not to thrust into her. I'd only had a few partners that were vampire kind in my years, but those experiences couldn't hold a candle to the overwhelming desire I was feeling now.

Her mouth opened and her teeth steadied against my pulse before she bit down. Her teeth barely broke the surface and she pulled away, licking the small line of blood that trickled out before the wound closed. She sat up, eyes closed, resuming her rocking motion as she savored the taste.

When she fixed her eyes on me again, her pupils were fully dilated and she ginned. "A little harder this time, I think."

I spoke with a shaky breath. "Yes."

She leaned forward again, still moving against me. Her teeth teased from my shoulder to my throat and rested against my pulse before she bit down. This time, she broke through with no problem. She pulled away enough to gasp as our joint pleasures surged, but neither of us finished. She drank and bucked against me as I thrust helplessly, but we couldn't find a rhythm in this position. It was excruciating.

She lifted off me, repositioning herself against the wall, on her knees. Her palms rasped against the thin plaster as I spread her knees wider, moving between them and sliding my hands over her hips.

My fangs grazed her offered throat and she brought my wrist to her mouth as I lined up at her entrance and drove inside. She gasped with every thrust, nails digging into the wall, sending plaster chips to the floor. My pace was feverish, both of us desperate. She met me thrust for thrust, slamming back into me, driving our pleasure higher as we reveled in our bond.

"Bite me," she begged, rolling her head back to look at me. I thrust hard and sank my teeth into her neck as she bit into my wrist. Stars burst across my vision with the force of my climax, and I only dimly registered Meg's cries of release as her own climax crashed over her. Our movements were automatic as we writhed, our energies flowing in a circuit as we became drunk on each other, only breaking away for periodic gasps and moans.

Finally, we came down, the intensity leaving our limbs weak and shaking. Meg turned her head for a kiss, and I tasted our blood mingled together before we sank back to the floor, barely having enough energy to crawl into the blankets and curl up around each other before we fell asleep.

The door banged open, and I jumped to my feet ready to attack, when I realized it was Gareth in the doorway.

"Gods, man, did you have to knock the door in?"

"I found him," he said, looking excitedly between us. "I found Remi."

Meg was on her feet in an instant. "Where?"

"There's a garrison, not too far from here. I overheard a conversation, and they mentioned his name." His face darkened. "Among other things. The sooner we get him out, the better."

The breakdown that Gareth gave us wasn't heartening. "How are we going to break into one of the most secure places in the city?" asked Meg.

I gave her a wry smile. "Just consider it practice for the main event."

She huffed out a laugh before her entire face lit up. "Wait. I know exactly how we're going to do this. We need to go undercover."

Gareth and I just gave her blank looks. The language lexicon wasn't much good for subtext.

"We go in with a disguise. Pretend to be something we're not."

I bobbed my head side to side as I thought about it, pretty sure I knew where she was going with this.

"The baron wanted a Stranger for his event," she said. "What if I go in there, telling them I was sent to arrange it? I can drop Montrose's name and the baron's, and move up the timeline so they prepare him to move before anyone would have the chance to figure out what we were doing. Maybe they won't even check. How many people would come around attempting this and dropping those specific names?"

I scratched my chin as I worked the idea over, cursing at my stubble. It was almost grown into a full beard now. I hadn't had a chance to shave in all our running.

Gareth was standing, arms crossed. His jaw ticked as he clenched it. He never did like the planning phase. It had to be tough for him not to rush to action, especially given it was one of ours in peril. "Didn't you say that horseman was being patronized by the king?"

He nodded.

"How can we be sure that man won't be there?" I asked her. "And recognize that you aren't a member of the court?"

Meg paused. "I can be visiting from a foreign country. Courtiers come and go all the time, right?"

I grimaced. "That's risky. What if he has questions about the court that you say you're from? Or maybe he's been there before himself."

That didn't seem to faze her.

"I know a fair bit about this time period. I should be able to get by under scrutiny."

"*Should* be able to?" growled Gareth. "You'll be walking into the middle of a garrison. Full of armed guards. We need to be damn sure of success before we send you in there, otherwise it's gonna be very difficult to get you out."

Meg looked at him with a flash of annoyance. "Sometimes taking a risk is necessary."

"He's right," I said. "We have to balance the pros and cons here. Even if you managed to convince them it's true, there's no guarantee, and in fact it's very unlikely, that they'll move him the same day. They would need time to arrange it, which means you would need to go back."

Meg's eyes lit up. "But's that's the key isn't it? I go in there, pretending to be a messenger, the new arrival that they sent in to deal with the task that nobody else wanted. Tell them that Remi is needed for the baron's party the next day and they need to get him ready. I don't put a huge sense of urgency on it, so it keeps their suspicions down. And if I appear nervous, well, I'm out of my depth as a visitor to court. That would be expected."

Gareth, and I exchanged a look. "It's not bad. I'm still not convinced that it's foolproof..."

"Nothing ever will be," she said. "If we've learned anything the past few weeks, it's that this whole thing is a shitshow. Nothing will ever go to plan one hundred percent. But one thing I am very sure of is that we're great at getting out of tough spots.

If something goes wrong, which it will, we'll find a way to deal with it. Of that, I have full confidence."

"Full confidence, and very little sense of self-preservation," said Gareth, shaking his head.

Meg's eyes unfocused, and a flash of discomfort went through the bond. "What's wrong?" I asked.

She shook her head. "Just a memory. Of Bel. I had a conversation very similar to this with him, right before I found the six of you." She frowned. "Back then, my lack of self-preservation was more of a joke. My how things have changed."

I could tell Gareth wanted to sidle up to her and wrap her in his arms, but he resisted to prove some kind of point to himself. I wondered how the original purpose of his walk had gone. Had he made a breakthrough with his wolf?

"Are you truly comfortable with this?" I asked her. "We'll support your decision, but if you have any doubts..."

A resoluteness hardened in her eyes. "I can do this."

Gareth huffed. "We know you can do this, and will do this. You're too stubborn not to." Meg gave him a sideways smile, which he returned. "But if you foresee any problems, we need to discuss them now."

Meg wrapped one arm around her middle and scratched at her elbow. "Honestly, if I think about it too much much, I'll talk myself out of it."

"Oh, that sounds like you're really confident. Let's go now," said Gareth, eyebrow peaked.

"I think better on my feet." She shrugged.

"You're not making either one of us feel better," I said.

She blew a strand of hair out of her face. "Shit. You're right, this sounds like a terrible idea."

I think Gareth and I both breathed a sigh of relief that she'd changed her mind.

Then she grinned. "But, we won't know how terrible until we actually try it."

CHAPTER SEVEN

Meg

I itched at the horrendously scratchy fabric of the dress Andrus had "borrowed" from a tailor on the wealthier end of the city. Brocade and lace with a high collar that tickled under my chin nonstop was making me more than a little irritable, not a good start when I knew I was walking into a situation that would put me face to face with people doing awful things to my mate in the name of *science*.

I'd always made it a point never to put myself in a position where I would garner attention, especially when I had to stick around in a place longer than I'd planned. Now all of that was going out the window, and my comfort zone with it.

The gloom of the dungeon was oppressive, settling into my bones. We walked through dimly lit corridors, thick with a horrible stench, the screams of the dying and those being tortured ringing harshly off the stone. The walls were grimy with slick mold, and there were puddles underfoot, intermittent splashing marking our passage as we moved deeper into the dungeon.

I thought the portrayal of these places in movies and TV shows was always exaggerated, but now I thought they didn't do it justice.

How long had Remi been here? They certainly wouldn't need charges to hold him on, not in this time. And his being a Stranger made it worse. They wouldn't even need to manufacture something like treason against the crown to make him disappear into a hole forever.

I hoped that Gareth and Andrus would stay out of sight and trust me to do this on my own. If they got jumpy, it could ruin everything. I needed to prove to them as much as myself that I didn't need their protection all the time. The guard stopped in front of the heavy panel door and when he knocked on it, the resounding noise told me it was wood over solid iron. Heavy steps trundled forward and a small latch in the door opened as the guard in the room beyond eyed us. The smell of blood was so strong I had to resist gagging.

The guards spoke in what I was coming to recognize as their customary language of grunts and pointing, and then the door swung open on surprisingly well-oiled hinges.

Remi wasn't the only one in here. Rage boiled to the surface as I saw the various contraptions and machines and devices that at least a dozen Strangers were bound to. A few of them were already dead, and the rest looked like they would gladly follow.

There were shifters caught halfway between forms, ugly looking clamps and hooks attached to the nonhuman parts of themselves. A magus of some kind was hanging from the ceiling, tongue and eyes missing. His arms hung toward the ground. His hands had been removed and the end of the stumps crudely cauterized.

A harpy that reminded me starkly of the Delphi Oracle was trapped in a cage, spikes holding her in place. Her teeth had been pulled, and her throat had been cut with surgical precision lengthwise, continuing their incision down through her sternum. They flayed open her skin and ribs to make a grotesque type of window. I gasped as I realized her heart was still beating.

A small weasel of a man dressed in an alchemist's robes was observing the various victims, studying the effects of these experiments. Could this have been the man that Gareth had seen? He prodded at the harpy's lungs and added a few forceps to her throat, exposing her vocal cords for further "study."

"Stop that," I snapped.

The alchemist turned, a look of surprise on his face. "What is she doing down here?" Far from being horrified that he'd been caught in the act, he simply looked irritated that I was bothering him. Now there was no doubt in my mind that he was the one working for the king.

The guard behind me spoke up. "She's looking for *him*."

The alchemist's eyes brightened with interest and suspicion. "Now what would you want with our most esteemed guest?"

I tried to maintain my bearing as a courtier, but my calm was evaporating. It took every amount of restraint I had not to attack them both and battle my way out of this dungeon if I had to.

"Baron Duval sent me to arrange for the beast's attendance at his next gathering. Tomorrow."

The alchemist sniffed. "I'm afraid that's not possible."

"Father Montrose directed the baron to you. I suggest you take it up with the priest if there's a problem. But the baron is insisting. He wants to make a big impression, the kind of party they'll be talking about for years."

The oily grin on the alchemist's face made me desperately want to wipe the floor with it. "Well, he's got the right idea there."

He motioned for me to follow him, and I had to skirt a large puddle of blood on the floor as we moved toward the back of the room. There was an even bigger door back here. All around the frame were sigils, the type of which I didn't recognize. They must've been of the alchemist's own making. I felt a heavy repellent pressure as we neared the door. The man motioned for the guard to open it, and as it swung back, I noticed the iron of this door was at least twice as thick as the other. They were also sizable dents, about the shape of a fist over the entire surface. Cracks and chips in the stone around the hinges were visible, broken away under the onslaught.

There was only one occupant of this room. The man had a shackle on both wrists and ankles, and each was attached to three chains. Each link was the size of my hand and twice as thick. The man's head was down, but I could see the slight rise and fall of his chest.

Any relief I felt that he was alive was short-lived.

His body was on full display, barring a shredded cloth hanging around his waist. He was horribly scarred. The deepest ones had straight, even edges, made with a sharp blade. Something bulged from underneath his skin where his clavicles met. It glowed and illuminated his skin from the inside with an odd greenish light and as I watched, that glow grew brighter.

The man stirred and lifted his head, and his eyes met mine. The object embedded in his skin flashed so brightly I was momentarily blinded, and the alchemist gave a cry of surprise, grabbing a heavy object off the wall that I only realized was a cudgel when he was within striking distance of Remi.

"No!" I barked sharply.

The alchemist paused and looked at me, curious. "I'm only subduing him, lady. It won't kill him."

I tried to recover my poise from my initial shock, hoping neither the guard nor this sorcerer had realized anything was out of the ordinary. "I just don't want you ruining the presentation."

The alchemist gave me a sickly grin. "I assure you, he heals fast. The baron needn't worry."

I gave him a warning grin, shooting daggers with my gaze, and attempting to keep my head tilted at a stately angle to maintain superiority. That haughty, better-than-thou persona made me feel slimy.

I motioned with a flippant wave of my hand. "Regardless, he seems to be posing no threat. It hardly seems like he's going anywhere."

Remi had stopped moving and was staring at me with such intensity that it broke my heart. It was a look that was telling me plainly to escape here as fast as I could. But he would learn just like Gareth and Andrus had that thoughts of my own safety faded when someone I cared about was in danger. I returned his look with one of my own, telling him I was not leaving him behind.

The alchemist busied himself bustling around the room, not noting our interaction. The guard was still hovering in the doorway, but he was a man they kept on the job for his brute muscle and not for his observational skills.

"There are a few tests that I need to complete before I can allow him to be transported. I'm assuming the baron will make all the necessary arrangements to guarantee security?" asked the alchemist, distracted with his notes and papers scattered around a workbench.

I'd taken a few steps toward Remi, his eyes still boring into mine, drawing me in like the proverbial moth to the flame. His eyes were cobalt blue, rimmed with thick black lashes. Thin Romanesque lips parted as if to speak. I crossed half the distance between us before I felt the guard's hand grab my upper arm. Whatever words Remi had been about to say turned into a snarl as he lunged against his chains. The alchemist turned in surprise and scolded me.

"My lady, it's much too dangerous to be near him. He's an animal. See how he's attempting to get to you? If he wasn't chained, there's no telling what he would do." He looked at the guard over my shoulder. "Escort the lady out, please."

The guard dragged me out of the room with Remi roaring and struggling against his restraints. The door closed with a thud. Sounds were muffled, but I still heard the impact of a heavy blow before it went silent.

Several minutes later, the alchemist reappeared. There were spots of blood on his face, and he looked hassled, wiping his hands on a rag. "Give me three days. My time sensitive work will be complete, and the baron can happily have his showpiece."

"The envoy arrives tomorrow. You can't have three days," I said coldly.

This flustered him. "I can't be expected to compromise such important work. The baron will have to make the concession. It's just another couple of days."

"If you'd like to tell him that yourself, be my guest. But it's also my understanding that the king will be in attendance. I'm sure he would like to witness what his money is housing."

The alchemist fidgeted. "I'll see what I can do."

I smiled, but it didn't reach my eyes. "The baron thanks you for your service."

The alchemist grumbled something and returned to Remi's cell, shutting the door behind him. My stomach clenched with worry, but he'd already survived so much. I had to believe one more day wouldn't make a difference. The guard herded me toward the stairs and out of the prison.

I'd relayed the entire ordeal to Gareth and Andrus immediately upon my return. Both of their faces were grim, and the fear and worry that we all shared was being compounded and amplified by the bond.

"When you show up without an armed retinue to transport him, won't that make them a wee bit suspicious?" asked Gareth.

"Maybe I can at least use the ruse to get them to unbind his chains," I said. "Make up some excuse about how the retinue assumed the prison guards would handle transport to the street?"

"Even if that does work, by the sounds of things, Remi wouldn't be strong enough to fight his way out if necessary."

Frickin' Andrus, always there with his logical reasoning.

"If I can get him to street level, that would even the playing field. Security on the upper floor isn't nearly as heavy. I'll send you a signal, and you can be the cavalry."

"This plan relies on a whole lot of hypotheticals. Do I really need to tell you this isn't a good idea?" said Andrus.

"What other choice do we have? Because if you have any other ideas, I'm all ears."

The three of us sat with that in uneasy silence. "We at least have to try. I didn't sense any kind of wards on the place that I couldn't escape from, so if worse comes to worst…"

"Really? There are no wards?" Gareth asked dryly.

I shrugged and looked at him sheepishly. "Not once you get outside the chamber where they're keeping Strangers."

Both men scoffed. "Meg, this isn't reasonable," said Andrus. "We have to find another way."

"We're running out of time! Do you just want to sit here with our thumbs up our asses until the Hounds catch up with us again?"

Gareth scowled. "I'd rather take my chances with them, than see you walking into a situation where you will absolutely be caught. We won't be able to get to you. They could do any number of things by the time we get there. *If* we get there. There are too many unknowns, and none of them work in our favor."

"I know I'm asking a lot. But you need to trust me." They opened their mouths to protest, and I cut them off. "Yes, it's your job to protect me. I understand that. But I've been running dangerous missions alone for years. I've had to break into prisons before, not to mention a labyrinth, complete with a minotaur. I've got more tricks up my sleeve than you're giving me credit for."

Gareth softened. "It's not that we don't trust you or believe that you can do this. It's that you shouldn't have to do this alone anymore. We're stronger together. Think about it from our perspective. If something happens to you that we could've prevented… if we lose you…"

"You're not going to lose me," I said.

"I already did!" Gareth shouted, throwing his hands in the air. "More than once!"

The raw emotion in his words cut right into my heart. "No." I moved to stand in the way of his pacing. "You didn't lose me. None of that was on you. The first time, Bel got the drop on us. And the second time, you were torn away from me because *I* messed up and couldn't control my magick. You couldn't have prevented any of that! You've done everything right by me and more."

"Then let me do my job. Let me keep you safe," he continued. "When I was stuck in that in-between realm, I could only feel your emotions through the bond."

"You could? I was completely cut off from you."

He nodded. "There were so many times where you were terrified or hurting. And when you thought you lost Andrus, the anguish that you felt drove me mad. I was absolutely helpless to do anything about it. That was almost worse than the tortures we suffered in our dreams at the hands of Hypnos." He cleared a stray strand of hair from my face. "Don't ask me to do that again."

I was at a loss for words. I'd never even thought to ask about it from his perspective.

"My wolf..." At the use of his pet name, Gareth's eyes locked on mine. I reached up, grasping his face in my hands. "I'm sorry. I should've realized." I kissed him. "But we all have another job that's bigger than us," I said, interlacing my fingers with his. "And we need everyone on our team when we get to the final task, whatever that ends up being."

I noticed Andrus had retreated across the room and was staring at the street below with his back turned to us to give us space.

"Please," I said. "Trust me to make it back to you. You've seen what I can do to protect myself and the lengths I'll go to for someone I love. Even if they get wise to the plan, I'm good at convincing people that I'm worth more alive than dead. If there aren't any axes available to chuck into someone's chest, I'll improvise."

Gareth barked a laugh and the tension in the room lightened. He gazed down at me with such tenderness it made my breath catch. "My task becomes harder every day. I was always prepared to protect you at the cost of my own life. But the thought of not getting to spend eternity by your side is becoming a constant fear." He shook his head and looked at our hands, lifting one to his lips and placing a feathered kiss on my palm. "I never expected to love you. It's been hard reconciling that with my sworn duty."

"I love you, too."

Our bond flooded with warmth and comfort and happiness, and I realized I'd never said those exact words. I'd said it in a roundabout way, but I'd never told him directly, in no uncertain terms.

"You have my heart and I'll give you my soul if you ask it." He smiled and leaned down to capture a chaste kiss. "You have ruined me completely, Megiste. And I wouldn't have it any other way."

CHAPTER EIGHT

Meg

When dawn came, I was just a bundle of nerves. In a few hours, we would either be leaving here with Remi or, well... we wouldn't leave.

As I approached the prison, I attempted to put my courtier mask back on and hold my head high. My heart pounded as I stepped through the gates and was promptly greeted by the guards. Or at least I thought that was what the customary grunts meant.

Success for this plan meant even more now. After I'd made so many assurances to my mates and Gareth had confided his deepest fear, failure was not an option, if only because I didn't want to hurt them.

Andrus had found a weakness in their security on the walls and had taken Gareth with him to attempt to steal guard uniforms. I watched them slip away with the hopes it wouldn't be the last time I'd see them. I was more nervous about going up against these maniacs than I was about Bel.

We took the same route as we did before, the same agonized cries and wails for mercy punctuating the silence like a fist to the gut. The alchemist was waiting for me at the top of the stairs leading down to his specialized torture dungeons.

"Where is your retinue?" he asked. "You need at least twenty guards to transport him."

"They are under the impression that your guards will bring the beast to the gate, where they will collect him." I tried to muster up every ounce of charm that I had to convince him of the next words. "They are organizing their force and will meet us to take custody in twenty minutes."

The alchemist grumbled and shuffled off, heading down the stairs and motioning for us to follow. He leaned toward one of the guards on the doors and whispered something in his ear before patting him on the shoulder and sending him off. It seemed so casual, but I didn't like it.

"Who are the guests of honor that the baron is so eager to impress, my lady? Besides the king, of course."

I sniffed. "Some old sods from England."

For a minute I thought I'd overstepped, playing the England versus France rivalry. The alchemist's face had twisted into such an exaggerated mask of contempt, I was expecting him to strike me down right there. But then he shrugged it off and continued walking.

"My apologies, lady. It must've slipped my mind."

Oh, no. My instinct was already screaming at me to turn around and go, but as I looked behind me, I could tell that wouldn't be an option. Not without a very good excuse. There were at least six guards lining the stairwell leading back up to the main floor. I didn't remember them being there the last time I was here, but maybe they were only preparing for Remi's transport.

That guard that he'd sent on an errand wouldn't have had time to gather a force yet, would he?

I tried to take a deep breath. I was overthinking it, that's all. Hold on tight to that mask and carry on with the ruse. In a few minutes, I'd have Remi and we'd all be out of here.

We reached the portion of the dungeons where the wards formed prickly-edged barriers that pulled at my skin as we walked through. These were just light ones, more deterrents than anything else. The real heavy-duty ones were coming up next.

I kept glancing at the guards as we passed and would surreptitiously sneak a glance at the ones behind, hoping I would see Andrus's or Gareth's face to back me up, if needed. So far, though, no luck.

When we entered the main dungeon room, where I'd seen most of his Stranger test subjects, the room was empty. All the cell doors were standing open. All except for Remi's. The floor had been cleaned, the cages cleared away.

"Are you preparing for something?" I asked him.

He waved his hand absentmindedly. "Removing the clutter. The less obstacles or potential weapons for this brute to use as he's being transported, the better."

"That still seems like an awfully long way to go for security's sake." There was a waver of fear in my voice, and I chided myself. Don't fall apart now.

"We don't want to take any chances. Not when a *lady* of the court is it stake."

He knew. I turned on my heel and darted back toward the stairs. There was no question that he knew. I just hoped I could find Gareth and Andrus before—

A guard tackled me to the ground and two more piled on top of me. I felt cold metal around my neck and tightness as it clacked shut. Instantly, all the energy drained out of me. I couldn't feel my wolf, couldn't touch the time stream, couldn't sense my mates. For all intents and purposes, I was human.

I caught a reflection in a polished silver chalice on a shelf. The collar around my neck was glowing faintly with green light, a large artificial stone of some kind placed in the middle from which the light was emanating.

"What do you think you're doing? This is outrageous!" I shouted.

"You can quit the act," he said, strolling up to me like he had all the time in the world and was afraid of nothing. He stopped a few inches away. "Montrose had already approached me about procuring some fresh blood by the time you showed up. He's eager to keep the baron on his good side."

I cursed inwardly. The Fates are on my side, but apparently Lady Luck hates my fucking guts.

The alchemist was still talking, but it seemed like a rant he'd gone on many times before. "That man never met a vice he doesn't throw himself into until he's buried up to his neck in it. He's weak. But those advisors of his have the right ideas. They convinced the king to fund this work." He looked around him proudly at his own kingdom of pain and suffering. "And Montrose can pay his debts when he hands over freaks that come to him to confess their fears that they have these powers they can't control." He grinned. "Those are my favorite. I can get creative with the dissection. See what activates a response from their abilities." A giggle bubbled past his lips. "It's always a surprise."

"You're insane," I said.

The alchemist shrugged off my character assessment and took another step toward me, his hot, rancid breath making me gag. "I have no idea what you are. I thought I could determine everyone's specialty, but you're a mystery." He grabbed my chin with dry, cracked fingers, his jagged nails digging into my skin. "It's going to be fun taking you apart. See what makes you tick."

He laughed, a high-pitched cackle that split the air. "You almost had me fooled, I'll give you credit for that. I thought maybe the baron had decided to go around Montrose. He was always hesitant to deal with me directly." He licked his lips. "I do take a lot of getting used to, my skills unsettle weaker minds. But your misstep was to bring the king's name into your ploy. A good attempt, but you underestimated how devoted the king is to this project. He wouldn't jeopardize it for the baron and the degenerate bourgeoisie he spends his time with. And he certainly wouldn't attend any of the parties the baron puts on. A quick check with my contacts at court made short work of your lies."

The alchemist circled me, appraising. "So, what are you? And what do you want with Remi?"

I stared at him for a long moment before changing tactics. "I was told to come here," I said. "There was a group of Strangers that accosted me. They demanded that I sneak in here. I don't know what they want with him, I don't even know who he is. I'm just a shifter that got caught in the wrong place at the wrong time."

"Don't lie to me!" the man shrieked, spittle flying from his mouth. He took a step back and breathed deeply, tucking his greasy hair behind his ears. "But I do believe you didn't come here alone." He looked at a man near the exit, dressed in a uniform with more ornate designs than the others. "Commander, find her accomplices."

He gestured sharply toward the thick iron door and the guards hauled me over. "Until you feel like sharing more information, you can keep the beast company. I have preparations to make. If you still don't want to talk upon my return..." He grinned at me and splayed his hands. "Well, I suggest that you don't find out the alternative." The door opened onto the yawning black pit. They tossed me inside, and it slammed shut behind me.

Everything fell silent. Just the occasional squeaking of a mouse or a long, lonely echo of someone's cry of pain, before I heard Remi stir.

"Is that you?" he asked. His voice cracked, hoarse from disuse.

"Yes," I said, carefully heading toward his voice while waiting for my eyes to adjust. The faint glow of the gem around my neck, combined with the object implanted underneath Remi's skin, was providing just enough light to make out shapes in the dark.

I stopped a foot away from him.

"Why did you come here?" he ground out.

"Why wouldn't I? We're not leaving you behind."

"Now we're both trapped." His tone of reprimand hurt me. "You said 'we.' Who else is with you?"

"Gareth and Andrus."

Remi cursed.

"But I don't know if they were caught. They were attempting to find another way in. With any luck, they realized I'd been discovered and escaped."

He laughed, a slow, groaning sound, combined with a wheeze. "Even if they did escape the guards, they won't go far if you're here. They'll undoubtedly make attempts to rescue you, which will fail and end with them caught or dead."

I was struggling to understand what was happening right now. My brain understood that the circumstances of our meeting were far different from the others, but I didn't expect him to be so angry. At least, not at me. Who tries to shame their would-be rescuer? No, it hadn't gone according to plan, but it's not over 'til it's over.

"I can see you're a big believer in having hope."

"Hope is for idiots. Hope makes people do stupid things," he replied, and I could feel his condescending glare, which rankled me.

"Aren't you a cheery ray of fucking sunshine?"

Another laugh, a little more mirth than derision, but still nowhere near genuine. "You cut right to the point, don't you?"

"Subtlety isn't one of my specialties, no."

"And neither is acting like a courtier," he said, a sneer in his voice. I could make out more details in the gloom. He had a swollen face from a very recent beating, and I could smell fresh blood. A sticky patch on the side of his head pointed to the source of the wound.

"It'll heal," he growled.

"How did you know that's what I was thinking?"

"Because you're a bleeding heart. I bet you have Gareth and Andrus both eating out of your hands. They were always too soft in my opinion, especially when it comes to *fate*." He ground out the word "fate" with such open disgust that I almost laughed.

"I can see why it would be confusing to you. You clearly don't even have a heart."

"Better that, than running blindly into a losing situation to save a woman that got *herself* into this mess in the first place. I know you understood when I gave you a message to leave. You chose to ignore it and now we're probably all going to die for it."

I refused to let him rile me up. "How did you end up here?" I asked, taking a seat cross-legged on the floor in front of him. I appraised him with a cool detachment. Maybe this was just a side effect of the situation he was in. There had to be some chance that over the last two-thousand years one of the Desma was bound to have changed from an upstanding knight in shining armor to a surly scoundrel.

"Does it matter?" he sneered.

I threw my hands up and slapped them down on my thighs in frustration. "I don't know, it just seems like we have some time to kill right now so I'm trying to make conversation. If you'd rather sit here in silence, you are welcome to it."

He seemed to take me up on that offer. I toyed with the shackle around my neck, trying to find any weakness in its make. Or at least trying to figure out how it worked. Not only was my magick completely cut off, but I couldn't feel Gareth or Andrus, and that was causing me more distress than anything else.

"It's their form of sorcery," murmured Remi.

"How did they do it?"

He gave an almost imperceptible shake of the head. "Pit demons came. They offered these men great power for their service, and then the humans gave themselves over as vessels."

He snorted with derision. "I'm not sure if it was willing on the sorcerer's part. But something else started to latch on to them, and work through them."

"Genuine possession?"

Remi growled. A man of few words.

"So it's a hybrid magick," I said out loud, trying to work through the problem without expectation that he would contribute to the conversation. "And I'm assuming this gem is the focus. It's almost guaranteed that it won't break by any method that I would have access to in here."

I could see a few things scattered on the workbenches clustered around the walls. I made my way around the room, peering closely at the items. Most of the alchemist's notes were gone and the ones that were left were covered in barely legible script.

"What do you think followed the pit demons through?"

No answer.

"We got a really heavy feeling around Notre-Dame. Seemed like a being with more power than a pit demon."

"The cathedral," he said, voice soft. Almost wistful. "A beautiful place."

"Very. But whatever is hiding underneath it..."

"Abomination," he said, the word ripping from his throat. "Something terrible came, and I couldn't stop it."

I stepped closer. "What was it?"

He shook his head.

"One of the Kings of Hell?" I'd met Lucifer before, so I was confident it wasn't him. But the energy of that place didn't match what I remembered of the Kings either. It felt more sinister, more unhinged.

"No. Chaos." His chains shook and his tone became angry again. "Why did you come back?"

"Chaos demons? Like Behemoth? Jörmungandr?"

"Yes," he said.

My chest tightened. Voice small, I asked, "They're real?"

The glint of his eyes as they met mine was his only response.

"Oh, boy." I leaned against a bench, knees weak. Why would I have expected anything else? Of course there were giant monster demons running around. And these wouldn't be your average mega-monsters, like a hydra. They were descended from the Ancients, like the Titans were, just a little farther removed. Ranking among the Kings of Hell in power, but with much less self-restraint. At least, according to the stories that I'd always thought were just that. Nothing more than make-believe.

However, it wouldn't be a problem either way if I couldn't get us out of here. I forced myself out of a doom spiral and kept exploring.

There were jars of questionable liquids that I wasn't even going to think about touching, and a few blunt tools that wouldn't be good for much in the way of defense or to pry this damn collar off me. But I took a couple of the more promising-looking pointy things and stuck them in my garter belt next to the small push blade that I hid high up on my inner thigh.

I'd been largely ignoring the hulking grouch chained on the far side of the room, but I could feel his eyes following me through every step of my exploration. I spoke without looking at him. "Are you attempting to make me to disappear with the strength of your withering gaze?"

There was a soft huff of breath, and he turned his head away. I just kept pacing circles around the cell, stopping every time I heard a sound in the room on the other side of the door. I hadn't heard any large-scale kerfuffle, so I hoped that my men were okay. At least for now.

The shouts and screams echoed less and less, and I wondered how late in the day it was. Quitting time for the torturers?

"You're going to pace a permanent groove in the floor." Remi's gravelly voice snapped me out of my preoccupied trance.

"They can send me a bill for the repairs."

"You should settle in. You're going to be here for a while." His tone was reprimanding again, and I lost my patience. I stalked over to him and stopped an inch away. I had to crane my neck back to look into his face as he was hanging from the ceiling, suspended by the chains. His face was stone as he returned my angry stare, his eyes like chips of ice gleaming in the dark.

"I'm just trying to do everything that I can not to fixate on how worried I am about my mates," I snapped. When I called them "my mates," Remi's pupils dilated, and his stare became even more hawklike then before. "You may not have a very high opinion of me, and I have no idea how much it'll matter to you when I say this, but those two men mean more to me than anyone. The circumstances that brought us together may have been designed, but if they were here, they'd agree with me that there is genuine love between us. It's all I can do not to break down right now. I have no idea if they're alive or dead, if they're planning a rescue, if they're going to do something really stupid and reckless."

I took a breath. "Even more stupid and reckless than this plan was, to save a man who doesn't even want to be saved. You seem to have forgotten the oaths that bound you together as brothers."

"Don't speak of things you don't understand," he hissed.

"To leave you behind would betray everything they believe in. They aren't capable of it. If I wasn't even a factor here, if you were being held somewhere and they'd been sent to find you, do you honestly believe they'd just call it quits because it seems impossible?"

Remi turned his head away, unable to answer because he knew it wouldn't be a convincing lie.

"I can't even imagine what you have suffered here. There have to be a million and a half reasons for you to be bitter and angry and callous. But don't you dare take your anger out on me for trying to ensure that you could join us, or on them for following me into danger. They're bound to protect me, but they're also devoted to preserving the family that you all started together. We already lost Arthur to my own blind foolishness. I'm not going to just walk away from another." I shot him a glare. "As tempting as it might be to let you wallow in your own self-pity."

It might've been my imagination, but I could've sworn there was a tiny softening in the angry creases around his eyes. But Remi said nothing. I turned my back on him and continued my pacing.

"What happened to Arthur?" His question wasn't angry as much as it was curious.

I smiled bitterly. "Belsioch sold me lies that I wholeheartedly believed." I turned to face him. "Then I sent Arthur to his death, thinking that *he* was the bad guy."

"Belsioch?" A sudden surge of rage had Remi staining against the chains. The cacophony of noise after so much silence made me clap my hands over my ears. He noticed my discomfort and settled.

The commotion had drawn attention, and I could hear guards moving outside the door. A small metal window slid open, and a face appeared on the other side of the bars.

The alchemist's voice broke into the room. "I do hope you're getting along in there," he jeered. "If you would bear with us for a little while longer. Word reached the baron and he has taken an interest." From the tone of his voice, I suspected the alchemist would be on the lookout for moles. "Expect a visit."

Remi gave an angry, bullish snort. The alchemist laughed. "Apparently the beast doesn't want his toy taken away from him."

I pulled a face and rolled my eyes, knowing the alchemist couldn't see me. With a final gloating laugh, the alchemist slammed the metal door shut. I heard the tramping feet of the guards move off into the distance.

"If the baron favors you, don't fight him. His parties are just drunken fools betting on Strangers, guessing what their magick is and enjoying the display of powers."

"How do you know? Have you been?"

He shook his head. "Vincent speaks of them often. He doesn't have a high opinion of the baron, as I'm sure you've figured out."

"Vincent?"

"The alchemist." He shifted his weight. "They would never let me out of this cage. The king gifted me to Vincent personally for his 'research.' Which is why you need to trust me when I say going with the baron is the only way to save yourself."

"That's right. Montrose made reference to you being a Marquis. You must've been a favorite of the king."

A low rumble echoed from his chest, which could've been laughter or a growl. Something told me that if we made it out of here, even after decades together I'd never be able to read him easily. Barring him being removed from the group for being a jackass.

"I was." The chains rattled as Remi shifted uneasily. "I'd helped his majesty avoid a nasty intrigue in court that would've ended his life. He rewarded me with title and status for uncovering the plot. It started with a minor allotment of land and the title of Duke, but after I availed myself to the court time and time again, my power grew. That all ended when the king discovered I wasn't human." Another rattle from the chains as he shrugged his shoulders. "You will leave this place, and you will survive. You'll have a chance to escape."

"But—"

"And you will forget about coming back here for me."

"Is there some reason that you don't want to leave this hellhole? I mean, there's masochistic tendencies and then there's just insanity. Which category do you fall under?"

Remi gave a small half smile. "Neither. I just know a lost cause when I see it."

"It's really too bad for you then. I have a soft spot for lost causes. And even if I think you're an asshole, I'm still going to make sure you get out of here. If not for your sake, then for Gareth and Andrus. They aren't going to leave you behind," I repeated.

"They will if you tell them I'm dead."

I hissed through my teeth. "What is wrong with you? I'm seriously starting to think you've got a few screws loose. If you don't give me a hell of a good reason for leaving you behind, other than the fact that you're an idiot, I'm coming back here to save your ass."

Remi was silent for so long that I continued pacing, thinking he was giving me the silent treatment again. When he finally gave me his answer, it was so quiet I almost didn't hear him.

"I have no desire to continue helping the Titans."

CHAPTER NINE

Andrus

We moved quickly around the side wall, blending in with the foot traffic. We did a full circuit of the perimeter before I decided on point of entry. The best shot was a low wall that only had one guard tower overlooking it. If we timed it right, those on the tower would be none the wiser.

"Think you can jump this wall, or have you gotten less agile in your old age?" I taunted Gareth.

In answer, Gareth waited until the guard's back was turned, and leaped to the top of the wall and down the other side. After a quick glance in either direction, I followed.

The interior was crowded with storerooms, barracks, and stables, making it easy for us to move around undetected.

"We're just looking for uniforms to steal, right?"

I nodded. "Unless we find another way in that would avoid us being seen altogether."

Gareth shook his head. "I don't feel good about this. I want my reservations noted."

I sighed. "You've made them known already, in triplicate. If anything goes wrong, you can say I told you so."

"That's not going to make me feel better if we're all dead."

I couldn't deny that my gut was twisted with worry. I had serious doubts about this plan working too, but there was no other option. This was the only way that we could be there to support Meg, because she was going to do this with or without us. I'm sure it was due in no small part to her continuing guilt over what happened to Arthur.

As I looked around, I could understand why she was so insistent on this plan. Storming the place wasn't an option, and if he was as tightly locked up as she said, there was no way we'd be able to get him free quickly. On the off chance that we managed to sneak into this place, it was highly unlikely we'd make it back out with him in tow. There were few options.

Gods, if Hadi was here, he'd be able to make one hell of a distraction to draw them out. A good old-fashioned dragon siege. Felix would've been able to craft a web of illusion, keeping us well hidden on our way in and out of the prison. I sighed. The hard truth was, Gareth and I were a shadow of what the Six had been at our full strength, and probably the worst two mates that she could've found first.

Without the rest of our team, we were stuck here with only our brute muscle, fully at the whims of others to determine our course of action. It was either they bring him out to us, or we wait until they move him. And unless they believed this ruse, it seemed highly unlikely they'd have another occasion to do so.

Even if we tried to burn the place down, they'd probably leave him behind, not to mention everybody else that was stuck in there.

If he'd had access to his powers, that would've been reasonable. He could survive fire no problem. But he didn't.

This seemed more and more hopeless the more I thought about it. Why couldn't we catch a break? Was there some kind of lesson buried in all this? A test?

Just beyond the next row of barracks, I made out Meg's form moving in between an escort of soldiers. Even though I knew she could protect herself, it still didn't help ease my worry, or the small inkling of possessiveness that was telling me to run over and force those men to move away from her.

The group disappeared inside the prison itself and the iron gate closed with a heaviness that punched dread into my stomach. I heard Gareth's furtive whisper and looked over to find him peering into the window of one of the storerooms.

"Andrus, come take a look at this."

I dashed over and stood just behind him, keeping half my attention focused on the guard towers. Then I noticed the sickening horror on his face, and I looked inside. Bile rose in my throat. "What the hell is this?"

Dozens of specimens were floating in hazardous-looking liquid, filling neatly labeled jars along the shelves. An aura of dark sorcery hung over the place, brushing up against my skin with a stinking ozone that left a bad taste in my mouth. The specimens looked... bizarre. Nothing about their form or shape made sense. I peered closely at the largest vessel filled with a dark-purple, viscous fluid in which a tiny shape floated, surrounded by several pairs of leathery wings. One pair was wrapped around the thing's body like a cocoon. It twitched, and I backed up a step, startled.

"That alchemist is a sick psychopath," I whispered. I was about to turn away, but something mounted to a far wall caught my attention. I gasped, mouth hanging open in disbelief.

"Gareth," I said, pointing.

"My gods," he breathed. He choked, retching, ducking down and trying to muffle the noise as he vomited. Remi's wings, still bloodied and jagged where they'd been cut from his body, were displayed like a trophy. And not just one pair. Three identical sets.

I backed away and scanned for our route forward. We needed to get out of here. All four of us.

I jerked my head for Gareth to follow, still wiping his mouth and looking green around the gills. A small group of guards was heading toward the front gate, and we waited for them to pass before darting ahead into the next patch of shadows.

We flattened ourselves against the wall of a long, low building and I peered in the window, inching my face around the frame in case there were any onlookers. It was a barracks, stuffed with soiled straw mats. They were empty, and we continued on.

There was an eerie stillness that didn't sit right. Maybe we caught it during a change of watch, but there didn't seem to be nearly enough movement for first thing in the morning. Maybe times were different now? In my prime military days, we were already halfway done with our duties by the time the sun was this high in the sky.

Gareth clearly felt the same unease I did. He shook his head. "We should tell Meg to get out. We'll reevaluate. I don't want to leave Remi in the clutches of these monsters for another second, but—"

There was a commotion, a quick movement of bodies toward the front entrance of the prison. "Shit," I said, backing away into the shadows.

"Do you think they figured it out?" There was a note of panic and his voice. "I didn't feel anything from Meg. Did you?"

"No. But she's probably in the warded areas," I reasoned.

A commander burst out into the courtyard. "Look for intruders! Anyone that doesn't look familiar, bring them to me!"

"We need to go," I said, grabbing Gareth's arm.

He resisted, jerking his arm out of my grasp. "I'm not leaving without her."

"We've been over this, we're no good to her if we're caught. We have a much better chance at rescuing her if we're free."

"But—" he protested again.

I grabbed both of his arms, my fingers digging into his flesh like a vise. "No. We leave. Right now."

He could hate me all he wanted, but he would realize this was the best choice.

Reluctantly, Gareth followed me back to the wall. We vaulted it and ran full speed toward our hideout.

It had been two hours, and we'd felt nothing from Meg. Gareth was pacing up and down the small space, running his hands through his hair. I could see his skin rippling periodically as his wolf fought for dominance to rise to the surface in his agitation. The low, constant murmur of his growl was an ever present sound in the room.

"Did you think of something yet?" he snapped.

I shook my head, but before I could say anything, Gareth lunged at me. "This is your fault!"

I backed up a step and put some distance between us, regarding him with my eyes lowered. The stakes were high enough without me inadvertently issuing a challenge to his predatory side. I didn't need to fight a wolf on top of everything else going wrong.

"We'll sneak back in tonight—"

Gareth crossed the distance and grabbed my tunic in his fists. "We can't wait that long! There's no telling what's happening right now. Why can't we feel her?" Underneath the anger was an overwhelming panic.

I still refused to engage him in a fight. I peeled his fingers off my tunic and once again backed away. "They won't kill her. I doubt they would dare do anything else either."

Gareth's eyes flashed yellow. "You have no way of knowing that for sure."

I inclined my head. "You're right. I don't. But we know the habits of people like this. This alchemist surely knows he's captured a special prize. He'll be evaluating, trying to figure out how she'd be most valuable to him. And the rumor mill is already running." I bobbed my head, making sure to catch his eyes. "The court will have heard about her by now. If either of us know anything about the elites, it's that they like to see curiosities with their own eyes. Who's to say the baron hasn't gotten word and wants a special guest at his party? I wouldn't be surprised in the slightest if arrangements were already being made. When someone shows up, we follow."

I braced a hand on his shoulder. "You know I'm right."

A desperate worry clouded his face. "There are plenty of other ways they could hurt her without killing her."

His words made me nauseous, but I took hope from what I knew she was capable of. "Do you not know our mate at all? Do you think she would let human scum touch her? Even if her powers were suppressed, she would fight like hell and do so much damage that they wouldn't try it again."

"You really believe that?" asked Gareth.

I nodded firmly. "I have to. She's survived a whole lot more. Let's find a new place to hide out, one with a better view of the prison. We should be able to get a better judgment on what's happening if we can see the traffic going in and out."

Gareth nodded. "There was a small granary, behind the bakery next to the garrison walls. It looked empty. It would provide a good viewpoint to watch the gates."

I allowed myself a small smile. "That sounds perfect. Let's go."

The sun was well on its way toward noon, the streets holding in the heat and making the smell so much worse. How had things have fallen so far from rational? I watched a herd of mice and rats scurry from one end of an alley to the other, fearlessly chasing a cat that bounded up a fence and onto a balcony to escape them.

As if that wasn't bad enough, when we opened the small latch to the granary door, more rats spilled out, flowing over our feet like water. I jumped back to let them pass before the two of us stepped inside and shut the door. There were small vents cut into the walls to allow air circulation. It would be perfect for concealing us while giving us a line of sight.

The heat became sweltering in the space, and I badly wanted to open the door for some extra ventilation but didn't dare.

I saw the alchemist return, jumping down from a cart and bustling into the garrison, his robes billowing behind him. I elbowed Gareth, who had been keeping watch on the other side.

"Our friend has returned. What do you want to bet he has news of someone coming to visit?"

Gareth gave a small smile, and I could hear a modicum of relief in his voice. "No bet."

Now it was just a matter of waiting.

We're coming, Meg.

CHAPTER TEN

Meg

I blinked, uncomprehending. "What do you mean?"

Remi couldn't even look me in the eye. "Just what I said. I have no interest in continuing with your mission. The Titans turned their backs on me, so I'm doing the same to them."

He didn't sound convinced of his own words. In fact, I got the distinct impression that he was purposely lying to me. "You don't mean that."

He grunted and fixed those ice-chip eyes on me again. "I guarantee you I do. So here's my advice." He took a breath. "When someone from court comes to take you, charm them, convince them that you'll behave, and use your first chance to escape." Remi's eyes dropped again. "And don't come back for me."

I shook my head and stepped forward, slippers silent on the filthy flagstones. Dirty straw scattered under my feet as I stopped right in front of him. He turned his head to avoid my gaze, but I reached out and grabbed his chin, turning his face back to me. "What is your problem?" I'd had it with his shit. I don't know what act he was trying to pull off, or if he thought it would make him some kind of hero to sacrifice himself, but I was done.

"You can't even convince yourself that you're speaking the truth, but you expect me to believe it?"

He bared his teeth in a sneer more akin to a grimace. "Believe it or not. I don't care. Just leave here and don't come back."

My fingers grip tighter into his jaw as he tried to extricate himself from my grasp. "Remi."

He closed his eyes to avoid my gaze.

"Remi," I growled. "Look at me."

Very slowly, he opened his eyes. His pupils were dilated, and even though he was trying his hardest to fill his eyes with hatred and scorn, there was a small bit of hope there too.

"I can't even begin to imagine what's happened to you here. And I'm sorry."

His eyes sharpened at my apology. "Why?"

"This shouldn't have happened to you," I said simply. "How long have you been here?"

He took a rattling breath, and I released his face. His jaw worked in a nervous tick as he clenched it, trying to work out how much of the story he wanted to tell me. "I'm not entirely sure. Sometimes it feels like an eternity. But I'm relatively certain that it's been at least five years."

My knees almost gave out. "Five years?" Rage and heartbreak swelled up within me. He'd been dangling in chains, suffering tortures and experimentation for that long? What was probably only a couple of weeks at most when I was being held and tortured by Bel almost broke me. Almost killed me. I wouldn't have made it another week let alone years.

I calmly placed a hand on his chest, and he flinched. I couldn't keep the tears out of my voice. "How can you think that you deserve this? Why would you want me to leave you here?"

"I want you to get away. I'm a lost cause. My shackles are ensorcelled. The only way you're breaking them is with that alchemist's magick. There is no other way."

"Never say never."

Remi scoffed. "Your well of positivity will run dry in this place. You don't know what you're up against."

"Then tell me."

"You don't listen!" he roared, lunging toward me with a clank of metal. I felt a small jolt of alarm but held my ground. "I already told you that demons are involved here, I don't know the specifics of their magick. You seem to think you know better than me, but you don't. Typical Titan egotism. You can't admit defeat, even when it's inevitable."

"There's only defeat if you give up. Forgive me if I refuse to do that."

From far away, I felt, more than heard, the echo of heavy doors opening and closing. The footfalls of a large group of people were moving this way.

"That would be your escort," said Remi. "Just do what I advised you to do. There may still be time to save the others."

I looked at him, disgusted with his attitude.

The grump was right. In short order, the small window snapped open once again, and the alchemist's watery eyes peered in to the cell.

"Girl, step forward."

I hesitated.

"Do it," said Remi. "Please." There was a raw vulnerability in his plea.

I did as I was told, shielding my eyes from the much brighter light as the door swung open and rough hands grabbed my arms and hauled me out into the main room. I hunched into myself and kept my eyes cast down. The hands pulled me forward and shoved me a few stumbling paces, causing me to trip and fall on the uneven stones.

There was a soft *tsk* above me, and very expensive looking shoes moved into view. The man squatted in front of me. Light fingers poised under my chin and tilted my face upward until I was looking into the cruel, calculating eyes of the baron himself.

I tried to hide the disgust on my face, pulling my chin out of his grip and burying my face in my shoulder. He chuckled, and stood.

"The rumors were true. A very interesting specimen, indeed," he said to the alchemist. "Well done."

"Thank you, Baron Duval." The simpering tone of the alchemist's voice made me cringe.

"Stand, girl," the baron ordered.

I pushed to my feet and wrapped my arms around myself, still keeping my face tilted away. Duval moved in closer until I felt his breath on my face. On the surface, he smelled of mint, but underneath it was rot and decay. "Would you care to accompany me to court?" The mocking tone made me want to punch him in the face, but I resisted. Barely.

"It would be my honor."

Duval seemed to think that that was a grand joke. He burst out laughing in a hearty guffaw, slapping one of his personal guard on the back. "The guests will love her. Bring her."

I cast a look back at the gaping darkness of the cell that hid Remi from sight, then turned my attention forward and followed the baron.

The carriage ride through the rough cobbled streets was surprising. I figured he would've put me in the back of the wagon, but he instead had me take the seat opposite him as we headed... wherever we were headed. We were going at a slow pace, both to account for thin wooden wheels versus uneven paving stones, and the need for his personal guard to fan out around the carriage on horseback as it moved.

I watched out the window, curious, and met the equally curious stares of passersby as they eyed the carriage. It was night, but this must have been a main thoroughfare. Torches lined the streets, and it was still bustling with activity.

The entire time I watched the scene outside the window, the baron was studying me. His fingers were steepled against his thin lips, the occasional hum vibrating from his throat. Finally, he spoke. "Did anyone inform you about my gatherings?"

Not taking my eyes from the window, I answered humorlessly. "Something about you and your degenerate friends—not my words, that was the alchemist—placing bets on people."

From the corner of my eye, I saw him incline his head. "Good. No need to explain, then. What are your abilities?"

I finally turned to meet his eye. Either Vincent hadn't told him what I'd said, or he hadn't believed me. "I'm afraid the alchemist made a mistake. I don't have any. I was the runt of my family, born mundane."

"Come now, don't play coy. All you freaks have your own powers, even subtle ones."

I bristled at his use of the word "freak." I'm very fond of that word, and didn't appreciate someone using it as an insult.

I turned away and stared out the window again.

The baron leaned forward into my personal space, the threat of danger radiating from him. "I will gladly hand you back to Vincent to do what he pleases with his—" Duval waggled his fingers carelessly. "—experiments. And you can also cut the shrinking-violet act. I haven't kept my position by being unable to read people."

Calling my bluff, was he? I leaned forward until my nose was an inch away from his. "Doesn't it defeat the point of guessing if you already know?"

"House rules," he said with a shrug.

"Fine. My secret power is..." I smiled and drew out the suspense until Duval's anger had built to the point of explosion.

"I can shift into a wolf."

He frowned. "That's it?" he asked. "A simple shifter?"

I shrugged. "You asked, I answered."

He leaned back in his seat and steepled his fingers again, going back to appraising me in silence. I continued my watch out the window and ignored him.

"I don't believe you."

I blinked. "Why would I lie?" I crossed my arms and legs, trying to resist the urge to fidget with the collar on my neck. It was getting itchy and hot.

"You are not like any shifter that I've brought into my home before. They always had a certain animalistic sense about them. You could tell them for what they were, even before you saw them change. You don't have that same sense about you."

"Should I be insulted?"

"On the contrary. I pulled you out of that dungeon because I want to put on a good show. Just tell me what you are. I can properly build up the suspense. Get them to part ways with more of their ill-gotten money."

"I'm a shifter. If you want proof, take this collar off me and I'll show you." I smiled dangerously.

"Not a chance," he said.

"Chicken."

He didn't rise to the provocation. He steepled his fingers against his lips. "If you don't cooperate, I will send word to the prison. Have them kill Remi."

I guarded my reaction carefully, hoping the shock hadn't shown through. "He means nothing to me. That's not really threat." I swallowed thickly. "From the looks of it, he'd welcome the reprieve."

"Cut the bull. You were attempting to save him. You didn't plan that entire ruse and just pick someone at random."

"Say that's true, I was trying to save him. Isn't he pivotal to the king's experiments? Seems like killing him would be a great way to get on the king's bad side."

"Did Vincent tell you that?" He scoffed. "He's been working away in that dungeon for years with no results. The king couldn't care less if Remi lives or dies. Vincent's most fruitful pursuits have been elsewhere. Except for that disgusting little alchemist, nobody will miss that creature if I have one of my people walk right back in there and stab him through the heart. Cooperate, and you'll be returned to him tomorrow. But if you do not play along, neither one of you will survive."

I lapsed into silence and stared out the window. The clack of the wooden wheels on the cobblestones filled the silence. Duval had a grin on his face as I contemplated my answer.

There was a sudden break in the line of horsemen surrounding us, just a small gap as one of the horses stumbled. Beyond horse and rider, I saw two familiar faces staring intently at me. It took everything I had to school my expression. Gareth was ready to charge the retinue, but I shook my head ever so slightly. I stared hard at Andrus and once again shook my head, willing them to trust me and back off. If they charged in, they'd probably be killed outright, and it would only take a moment for word to reach the prison.

Andrus reluctantly nodded and placed a hand on Gareth's shoulder. My wolf looked sharply at his brother in arms, then back at me. Andrus turned away, shoving Gareth in front of him and leaning close to speak into his ear. My heart broke as I watched them disappear into the crowd. It only took a few seconds for that transaction, and then the horseman regained his place in line, and we carried on.

"Fine. What do you want me to do."

CHAPTER ELEVEN

Bel

"Have you found a good candidate yet?" I asked Risha. She was less skittish now, and I'd let her take Ursal back to their family. I was nothing if not generous. Her discovery had changed everything, and even if I was upset that it had taken her so long to share it, it still deserved a reward.

She motioned to a map projected on the wall. "These are the ones that look most promising." She clicked a button and dozens of small dots of blue overlaid the map. "And these are the places where he stays the longest, presumably because he has some kind of homestead there." She clicked the button again, green dots overlaying the blue. There were several similar points.

I looked at her curiously. "Why would you pick out those points?"

"I figured if we could find any commonalities with places that he's most likely to frequent, it would give him an even stronger tie to that place and allow you to bind him tighter."

A dark chuckle escaped me. "When did you become so devious? I must've had a good influence on you."

Distaste flashed across Risha's eyes, just a flicker which she quickly hid away. Instead of being angered by this display, I simply found it more endearing. She didn't want to help, would've left if I gave her the opportunity, but she was still doing very good work. That almost meant more to me than loyalty. She was staying not because she respected me, but because she feared me, and the power that I had over her even without her brother present.

"This is the sigil I think we should use," she continued, clicking the button one more time. A large shape overlaid the majority of the points, placing the epicenter right in the middle of a rune of binding. That rune was incorporated into a complex sigil that I recognized various components of, but not the whole.

"This sigil is of my own design," said Risha, a note of pride in voice. "It combines binding techniques from several different traditions across the globe. I figure at least a couple of them have to have a chance at slowing him down, and combined, they have a good chance at keeping him bound."

She stood and crossed to the screen, tracing her finger along the lines. "If we place teams at these various points, we'll have enough coverage. The essence of the sigil will be preserved and with you powering it, it should give it just enough juice."

"This is Death we're talking about. A primeval force. He won't go quietly. 'Just enough' is inadequate."

"Then maybe you shouldn't do this at all."

My eyes narrowed. "I'm sure you misspoke just now."

Risha stared back at me, defiant. "My lord, if you trap him, think of the repercussions. I know it's part of the offer that you made to the Hounds, but is it really worth it? Call them off, before they finish the job. You have the keys, you can find Meg yourself."

Even as she said that last sentence, I could tell she hated herself for it. She was still loyal to Meg, no matter what she was doing for me. But apparently her conscience cared more for the world large at the moment.

"The reapers are more than capable of picking up the slack. And eventually, they will find a new king to lead them."

"But Death holds so much of that force within himself. There would be no balance anymore."

My words were ice, thin and dangerous, ready to drag her down if she trod too heavily. "You dare to question me? Still, after all this? After I allowed you to take your brother away from here, after I allowed you to *live*, you still dare to question me?"

"Not at all. I'm simply imploring you to use your own power, and not to rely on those creatures. You are more than capable of it."

My eyes widened at the double-edged comment. Praising me, whilst also being condescending. She was certainly learning to weaponize her words. She's always been such a bookworm, I didn't think she had it in her.

"You forget, they are still hidden from me. That damn Oracle made sure they couldn't be tracked," I said, rolling my shoulder as a phantom pain from Apollo's arrow struck me all over again.

Risha didn't have an answer for that one. Before I could snap, I walked away. Over my shoulder, I said, "Get it finished. I want this trap ready to be sprung by tonight."

"Tonight? But—"

"Just get it done!"

I had preparations of my own to make.

The subbasement of the lodge was a hive of activity. Every nephilim at my command was waiting for their orders, having been split into groups of two by Risha. She was handing out the focuses—no longer brass keys, but a mélange of things she'd found around the lodge and surrounding woods that were small and compact enough to carry easily.

"Each of the focuses has coordinates written on it and a date and time. Once you speak the activation words, you need to read off the information as written. The portals will open, you will step through and you will not stray more than twenty feet from that location. Is that clear?" she asked.

A chorus of voices answered.

"If you need to conceal yourselves for any reason, and there isn't a place within twenty feet, bury this focus at the site where it won't be disturbed. Is that clear?"

Another round of affirmatives. Risha handed me another focus. "This one has been keyed to all of these," she explained, motioning behind her with an absentminded wave of the hand. She fished a remote out of her pocket and clicked it, displaying the map on screen.

"When master Belsioch activates his focus, all of yours will sync. The binding will activate and the trap will be sprung. Once that happens, Kirthe will move her team in for the capture. They will remove Death to our facilities here—"

"No. I have another place in mind," I said.

Risha simply nodded. "Kirthe, if you would consult with master Belsioch, I'll finish up here."

Kirthe complied and I led her away from the group.

"Where am I taking the prisoner, my lord?"

I handed her another item, a special key. "This will bring you to the dungeons. I've set them up within the mountain, separate from here."

"My lord?"

I waved her away. "You don't need to know more than that. Detain him and deliver him to me. I'll take care of the rest."

"Yes, my lord," said Kirthe, bowing at the waist. She returned to the meeting, which was just wrapping up.

"Are you ready, my lord?" called Risha.

I stared at the map and the many points across it, overlaid with the sigil. I nodded. "Go."

Each team activated their focus and spoke their specific coordinates. The light blasting from that room was searing, and once they'd all stepped through their gates, they snapped closed, leaving only a thin vertical line that pulsed with that same light.

Risha looked at a timer before glancing at me, the hatred no longer veiled. "Death should be arriving any moment. Kirthe is placing a significator near the site of the massacre that will send you a signal when he gets there. You can spring your trap and be done with it."

I smirked. "This is quite a change in you. Who would've thought our little Risha would grow a pair?"

"You're not mad?" she said, quirking an eyebrow. "This isn't threatening your fragile ego?"

I laughed. "You've done your job, and done it well. This is the guilt talking, that you're feeling for betraying your friend." I took a few steps in. "Once the Hounds deliver her and the rest of the Six, it'll be over." I leaned down until I was an inch from her face. "I'll make them beg for death." I barked a laugh. "But he'll already be there!"

Risha didn't flinch. "I hate you," she hissed. "I hope Meg kills you." She smiled. "But not until after she's torn apart your entire legacy so the world can see you for the fraud you are."

Now she'd gone too far. My breath stilled as my eyes narrowed and I clenched my fists ready to strike. A small light in the corner of my eye caught my attention.

"That'll be the signal," said Risha, backing slowly away.

"What are the activation words?" I asked.

A slow smile worked its way across her thin lips. "Down with the king."

"I will deal with you later," I promised before straightening. "Down with the king," I repeated.

Magick bloomed from the focus, and I honed it into an arrow that split and shot through the ether. I felt the other focuses connect and call back until there was an electric buzz that snapped into place like a shotgun blast. The sigil activated and the roar of magick tore through me. I held up my hand, palm up, fingers splayed wide and when the power was at maximum, I clenched my hand tight into a fist.

The trap snapped closed and I smiled as I felt the fly struggle, caught in my web. Death was mine. "I'll send word to the Hounds."

The special location I'd set up was in a pocket realm, much like the one I'd sent Arthur to, but without the menagerie of creatures to contend with. The rooms I'd prepared weren't uncomfortable either. In fact, once I entered the main chamber, I settled on a plush chaise lounge to converse with my captive.

Death was leaning casually against a wall in his cell. It wasn't a cell by human standards. I'd made sure to stock it with lushly upholstered furniture, there was plenty of room to stretch out and stroll. Everyone needed to stretch their legs. I had a servant on-site that would bring him whatever he would like as far as food and drink. He was free as a bird to do as he wished within his space. He just couldn't leave it.

A slow grin spread across his face. He still looked the same as I had seen him last time.

"We meet again so soon," he said. "I had no idea you enjoyed my company so much."

"It's my honor to host you here. And the Hounds will also be pleased to see you." There was no point in trying to hide anything. I propped my chin on my hand. "What's it like?"

"What 'it' would you be referring to?" His casual demeanor still hadn't changed.

"You knew this would happen, you had me figured out from word one, didn't you?" I spread my hands. "But you were helpless to stop it. What's it like to feel that way?"

Death moved, graceful and catlike, as he waltzed up to the bars. He wrapped his fingers around them and leaned in, never taking his eyes off me. "What makes you think I was helpless to stop it? Maybe I wanted to be here." He smiled wider. "You're right, though. I had you figured out from the beginning. I'm sure your powers of manipulation are quite developed, but it takes a lot more than that to fool me. Besides," he said, leaning back with a wrinkle of his nose, "the Hounds always piss on their territory. You belong to them now, and everything else you do will be a predictable result of that fact."

I couldn't stop the small inkling of doubt that creased my brow. "I belong to no one. Nobody has the power to rule over me."

"Keep telling yourself that lie," said Death, returning to his spot leaning against the wall. He picked at his fingernails. "Maybe someday it will become truth." He winked at me. "But I doubt it."

"You stand there and talk about lies, and you expect me to believe that you chose to be here of your own free will?" I stood, pacing toward his cell.

"I'm very confident that things around here are about to get quite entertaining, and I'd hate to miss it." That shrewd, knowing grin was firmly planted on his face, and I desperately wanted to wipe it off. He had to be lying. There's no way he could've outsmarted me. And even if he had something planned, this place was locked down. The only way anyone could access it is if I gave them permission explicitly.

He was powerful to an extreme, but if he planned on taking me on alone, he still could do nothing from that cell. He was just trying to get into my head.

"If that was my goal, looks like I've already accomplished it."

Had he read my mind? Or was it another trick?

"That's got to be a new record for me. It's only been, what? Two minutes, since you've stepped foot in here? And I'm already breaking down your confidence." He crossed his arms and tilted his head with an undeserved arrogance.

I was at the bars in a heartbeat, staring him down with my hands clenched around the cold iron. "You think you have me beat, but I assure you, you don't even know what game you're really playing."

"Spoken like a true defensive psychopath," Death said. He stretched and paced over to the armchair. "Send that servant in here, will you? I'm feeling peckish."

The iron under my fingers groaned as it bent from the tight clench of my fists and I had to tear myself away. I forced myself to slow my pace as I left the chamber. I didn't want that prick to think that he had me running, because he didn't. He had no power here. None. And I would prove it to him.

Chapter Twelve

Meg

I noticed the general improvement in the smoothness of our ride as the roads became better graded. A lush green expanse started to replace the cramped city center, and soon we were in the countryside. We reached the gravel driveway that led to a palatial country home, lit up brightly against the night. My heart was in my throat, pulse pounding painfully against the shackle around my neck.

I was so far away from being able to easily escape, to lose myself in the crowds. Trying to run out here, especially if I couldn't shift, would be a disaster. They would track me down in an instant once the sun came up.

As the carriage came to a halt, the head butler approached, giving the baron an oily smile before giving me a small glance and wrinkling his nose, like he had just witnessed a splotch of dirt on his pristine white coat. "Welcome back, my lord. I hope you find everything to your liking."

"Thank you, Pierre." Duval dismissed the man and turned to me. The butler looked slightly put off, but retreated nonetheless, barking orders at the others who cleared out quickly, heading back to their posts.

"Afraid that I might try to escape, bringing me all the way out here?" I asked him, even though that had been exactly what I'd been planning.

"You and every other freak that I've hosted here," he said, tilting his head up and looking down at me across his thin, long nose. His heavily oiled hair shone in the moonlight that glinted weakly through sporadic cloud cover.

As we turned to the house, a heavy patch of clouds rolled over the moon, making it look like a scene from a regency-era horror movie.

The servants gave us curious stairs as the baron ushered me through the large double doors leading into the home. It would've been beautiful under any other circumstance. As we entered, it was a feast for the eyes. There was so much gilt finery everywhere. If I thought the cathedral had been ornate, it was nothing compared to this.

Duval was appraising me as I looked around, his cruel sneer returning. When I saw it, I paused. What was he planning now?

"Would you care to see your accommodations for the evening?" he asked, his tone light, but his eyes cold.

My fists clenched and I wished that I could call for my claws. Being unable to access my most reliable weapon made me afraid. And then angry because I was afraid. I truly was as helpless as any average human in this state.

I nodded, but said nothing. The baron sniffed, once again holding his nose aloft in the air as he led the way farther inside.

The butler that greeted us approached. "Are you sure you wouldn't care for me to show... our guest to her quarters, my lord?"

"I already told you I had it, Pierre. Do you think me incapable?"

Pierre faltered and paled, stammering out his reply. "No, not at all. My apologies, Baron." He bowed low and backed away.

"You really have them scared, huh?" I asked.

Duval appraised me out of the corner of his eye. "I've always suspected Pierre has a soft spot for those... less fortunate... that I host here. If I'm assuming correctly, he was more worried for you than he was about making me comfortable." As he finished that sentence, he looked at me full on, gauging my reaction. Looking for my fear.

I wasn't going to give it to him. "And how many *less fortunate* have you had here?"

"Had or hosted?" he asked, his hand running down my back and resting on my ass. Immediately reacting, I shifted my weight, pivoting and striking out with my fist, nailing him right in the sternum. The hit was far weaker than it would've been under regular circumstances, but it got my point across.

Duval let out a surprised exclamation of pain, falling to his knees and coughing violently as his heart tried to regain its normal beat. His guard were on me in an instant, throwing me to the ground and pinning me. I watched the baron struggle to his feet as best I could with half my face pressed into the floor, grinning wide.

His face was contorted with rage, and I laughed. I may have been just a human, but so was he. Without his lackeys to come to his aid, he was no match for me. And now he knew it too.

"Take her to the dungeon. Toss her in the pit," he spat, turning on his heel with a furious toss of his hair. He turned back to add, "I need to decide if I'm going to send a message to the prison."

My smile disappeared and he was the one that got the laugh. He strode quickly away, people dashing to the side to clear the way.

The guards marched me down a dark, damp set of stone stairs. This place was more on par with the classic Hollywood dungeons. It was much smaller, and I was the only "guest" at this time. The two guards that I was suspended between dragged me to a far corner and pulled back an iron grate in the floor. The squeal as it moved on its hinges set my teeth on edge.

What greeted me was a dark pool of still water, a slick of something oily resting on top. They unceremoniously tossed me in and I closed my eyes and mouth a split second before I hit the cold pool. The grate slammed back down and the telltale click of a lock sealed me in.

The guards walked away, laughing. It was too deep for me to reach the bottom, although I could feel my toes scrape against it occasionally. At least I didn't have that horrible sinking feeling that something was hovering below, waiting to nibble at my feet. The walls, too, were very close, leaving me just enough room to spread my elbows to either side.

I wrapped my fingers around the iron bars and held my head above water, trying very hard not to think about how many other people had stewed in this pit, steeping like tea. Hell, most of it probably wasn't water anymore, but thinking about that only made me want to vomit so I steered clear of those thoughts. He wouldn't have Remi killed, I decided. It would remove any incentive for me to cooperate.

To distract myself from the worry, I instead turned to planning my escape.

I lost track of time since I'd been thrown in here, and my fingers were numb. All I knew was that the sun had come up at some point. My whole body was shaking from the cold when footsteps descended the stairs. Duval came into view, dressed to the nines and flanked by guards.

There was a glint of triumphant arrogance in his eye as he looked at my pathetic form, shivering, and clinging to dear life. "Your evening could've gone so much differently. The guest suite is very comfortable, although you likely wouldn't have wanted to leave my bed. And I would've given you your own maid to see to your needs during your stay. But instead, here you are." He wrinkled his nose. "Soaking in filth."

"You tried to change the terms of our deal," I said through chattering teeth. "I was willing to help you impress your guests. I was not willing to be less than impressed by you, in your bed."

A direct hit. A cold fury seeped across his features as his fists clenched at his sides. The guards stepped forward, ready to do his bidding, and punish me further for my transgression. The baron held up a hand to stay them. "No. There's no time for that. My friends have arrived, we need to get her ready for the show." He snapped his fingers and turned on his heel, a move that must've been a favorite of his for all the practiced grace of it. "Bring her."

The guards unlocked my cage and pulled me out of the fetid water, turning their heads away. I couldn't blame them for that one. I'm sure I didn't smell the greatest.

Even the cold, dank dungeon felt warm, and my shivering soon ceased. They dragged me up the stairs, servants moving to follow as they mopped up the trail of water cascading off me. It was already close to evening. Time flies.

I was taken to what must've been the servant's quarters, and thrown into a metal tub full of lukewarm water. Both guards stood by and stared lasciviously as I peeled off my dress. A small, meek girl wearing servant's garb approached with soap and a sponge, handing them to me before scurrying away. I washed quickly, realizing that this was the first proper bath I'd had since Norway. Although the two men I was with that time were far better company.

When the water was brown from grime, and I'd scrubbed every inch of my body, the girl appeared again with a towel and helped me step out of the tub. She pointed to a thin slip of a dress laid out on a chair before disappearing once again. I wrapped the towel around me and moved to the privacy screen set up in the corner, but one of the guards tsk'd.

"Stay where we can see you. Don't want you getting into trouble, after all," he said with a grin.

I bared my teeth at him, vowing to rip their throats out if I had the chance. I dried and dressed quickly, and the girl popped up out of nowhere, guiding me to a chair before doing my hair up in an elaborate fashion. She painted makeup on my face and anointed me with a perfume that smelled seductively musky. I caught my reflection in a polished silver mirror and almost didn't recognize myself.

It wasn't that the makeup was overly heavy, but since I never wore any, it took me by surprise. And I was amazed at the fineness of the hairstyle, all elaborate pin-curls and a braid wrapped around the mass of my hair piled on top of my head.

The chamber maid smiled at me sheepishly, and I returned it. Regardless of the reason, she'd done a very good job. Her smile faltered as the door opened and the baron stepped in, stopping in appreciation as he caught sight of me. "Very good." His eyes roved over me, head to toe. "One last chance to tell me what you are."

"Is Remi alive?"

His nostrils flared. "As far as I'm aware, yes. I have done nothing to him anyway."

"And you didn't send anyone after him?" I was staring him down, using his semantics against him to catch any sign of a lie.

"No," he sneered. "I didn't. Happy?"

I nodded. "I'm a demon. I can shift into a wolf, but I also have vampiric qualities."

"Was that so hard?" He turned to leave, but I stopped him.

"Remi stays alive, or you see none of it."

The baron didn't grace me with a response and disappeared down the hall, the set of his shoulders tense.

The guards moved forward, only one of them grabbing my arm this time. His grip was lighter on my bare skin, careful not to leave marks. I'm not sure why that would matter, but I wasn't going to nitpick.

They led me through the house, past a large dining room full of servants bustling away as they cleared the remnants of a feast from the table. Large windows made everything feel open and airy. Outside, the setting sun showed gardens in full bloom, the lawn finely manicured.

Across the wide, open parquet floor to the back of the house, floor-to-ceiling windows looked out onto yet more gardens, including a hedge maze. I'd never seen windows this big in a medieval home. I'd underestimated the funds the baron had at his disposal. The more money a man like this has access to, the more dangerous he was. There could be any number of unpleasant surprises waiting for me upon my escape.

We headed toward a ballroom. The conversation dimmed when we walked in and dozens of pairs of eyes fixed on me as they marched us down the long room, where Duval was waiting at the end, sitting on a less ornate version of a throne. He chained me to it, shackling my ankle on a long expanse of iron rings that gave me a good range of movement while keeping me thoroughly under Duval's control.

"My esteemed guests," he began, rising to his feet. "Before you, I have brought a new specimen for your appraisal. Most of you have already met our former Marquis, Remi, now sadly fallen from grace." There were titters of laughter around the room. "This woman made a very ill-advised and poorly planned attempt at *rescuing* him."

More laughter.

"I have brought her here this evening for the night's entertainment. As usual, you will all have time to study our guest and place your wagers on what you think her specific abilities are." He clapped his hands together in three smart raps, and a door opened to the side. A large cage was dragged out into the center of the floor.

All around it were carved runes and sigils of binding, and a pit of dread settled in my stomach as I realized I would be able to transform within that cage, but not escape it.

None of this was going according to plan.

"Let the games begin." Duval threw his arms out wide and mockingly bowed to the thunderous applause of his guests.

Chapter Thirteen

Meg

Several curious courtiers approached immediately, surrounding me in a small group as they talked among themselves like I wasn't even there. I was poked and prodded, my arms raised, my back examined. The entire time, they exchanged comments and furtive glances as they devised their guesses.

Once they were done, another group replaced them, and so on and so forth for the entire evening. Not once did any of them speak to me directly, or even look me in the eye. I wasn't human, so I didn't deserve to be treated as one.

One of the lords returned after everyone else had studied me, drunk and without the group he'd initially been with. Most of the other courtiers had gone back to mingling while they waited for the appointed time where I would reveal my secrets.

"Can you give me a hint?" he asked, a lazy smile on his face.

I blinked in surprise. This was the first time someone had spoken to me directly and for a minute I assumed there was a person behind me that he was speaking to. A quick glance over my shoulder proved that not to be true.

When I didn't answer, he leaned closer. "I really need to win this bet. Just tell me what you are, and I'll put in a good word with the baron. Maybe he'll let you go."

I laughed. He looked confused and his face fell. "You have influence over the baron?"

"My star in court is rising much faster than his these days. I might even be able to speak with the king himself on your behalf."

"Lawrence, you wouldn't be trying to cheat, would you?" asked the baron, sliding his arm around the man's shoulders, elbow hooking around Lawrence's neck, threatening.

"I can't believe you would assume I would do such a thing," he said, grasping at the baron's elbow.

Another courtier came up alongside the men. "Why don't we just close the betting and get on with the reveal? Before these ruffians can dig themselves into holes deeper than they already have."

The long-standing animosity between Lawrence and the baron was clear as they flung daggers at each other with narrowed eyes. I'm sure the copious amounts of alcohol all of them had consumed tonight contributed. This place was an aristocratic powder keg ready to blow.

I laughed as the image of a grand dame's powdered wig blowing off her head in a shower of white dust came to mind.

The room went uneasily quiet as stares were leveled in my direction. I held up a hand and waved in silent apology, although maybe I should've just kept laughing. Nothing is more terrifying than someone laughing for no reason at all, especially if they're shackled.

Charles motioned to the guards and they trudged over, unchaining me only to shove me in the cage and close the door. My hairs stood on end up and down my arms. The energy was ricocheting off the bars with such intensity that it felt like I'd walked into a wall of static electricity. My skin prickled, almost to the point of pain.

A guard reached through the bars and undid the collar around my neck, pulling his hands back and scurrying away. The first thing I did was try to reach out to my mates, to try and feel them. But no such luck. This cage trapped everything, including mate bonds, within its confines.

The fine, upstanding citizens crowded around, vying for the best view.

"Has everyone placed their bets?" asked Duval.

They were nods and general murmurs of agreement. He clapped his hands. "Perfect. Then, madame," he said, addressing me, "kindly show us your powers."

I stared back at Duval, sighing, before removing the dress and transforming into my wolf. There were general "ooo's" and "ahhh's", but as I fixed my violet eyes on the baron, he looked far less than pleased.

As polite applause sounded from the guests, and several of them crowded closer still to get a good look at me, the baron forced a cold laugh from his throat. The danger in it caused all his friends to blanch and turn in his direction.

"That is a wonderful trick, truly a lovely lupine specimen. But I know you are capable of much more."

The guest's turned back excitedly, expecting more to the show. I shifted back to my human form and dressed. "Maybe you should learn a little patience, yeah?"

I called my fangs forward and bared my teeth.

"Do your eyes change, too. We've seen that with other vampires."

I looked at the woman who spoke blankly. "Stick your arm in here and I'll show you. It only happens when I feed."

She laughed nervously and the others joined in.

Duval moved close to the bars, reaching through them, and grabbing hold of my arm to pull me close. "A minute, friends."

They all dispersed and he whispered so only I could hear him. "I'm expecting a show. Remi's life is still in my hands. If you're a demon, prove it."

I smiled. He'd just handed me my chance. "If you want to see the full display of my powers, you need to let me out of the cage."

His laugh was much heartier this time, almost a guffaw. "You must be insane if you think I'm falling for that."

I shrugged. "It's just how my power works. I can bend time, and to do that I need to be able to access the *flow* of time. This cage cuts me off from everything."

Duval's attention became much keener. "What does that mean? Bending time?"

What would be the best way to sell it to a narcissistic aristocrat? "In the simplest terms, I can turn back the clock. Or turn it forward. I can make people younger or older. I can make plants grow, or shrink into seedlings." I had his attention now. The wheels in his head were already turning with all the ways he could implement this power, not the least of which I'm sure was turning back the clock on those gray hairs of his.

The more I thought about it, the more I wondered if I actually could do those things. It would make sense. Just the same way that I'd healed Gareth, manipulating the movement of time in a select region of space should theoretically be easy.

"I've never heard of this power," he said, licking his lips.

"You wouldn't have. It's not something that we like to brag about. I'm sure you can see why we don't want people to know."

"What guarantee do I have that you won't just turn us all into piles of dust?"

A fair question. "If I could do that, don't think I would've done it already? With the guards back at the garrison?"

"So how does it work?" he asked.

"I focus on something specifically, and work my magick around it. I could go into more detail, but you wouldn't understand," I said with a snide grin that got his hackles up.

"Very well." He motioned for a guard to step forward. "Take her out of the cage."

The guard nodded and reached through the bars to put the collar back on me. "Without the collar," he said, lifting his chin confidently.

The guard only stared in confusion at the command.

"Do as I say!" barked Duval.

The man jumped into action, unlocking the cage and pulling open the door. The flow of Time rushed in and surrounded me in a whirlwind, and my connection to my mates snapped back into place. My hair whipped around me, caught in the stiff breeze and I delighted in watching Duval's eyes widen as he realized he'd made a mistake.

He backpedaled to get away from me as fast as possible, and several of the courtiers followed his example.

Gareth and Andrus answered my call, surging forward through the bond. They weren't far, they'd followed the carriage here.

Having my abilities locked away seemed to have made them stronger. In one instant, I was looking at a hall, full of scared aristocrats, and in a single blink, I was looking through the eyes of one of my mates.

I could see their surroundings and when he turned his head, I saw Andrus looking back at me. So I was seeing through Gareth's eyes. Both of them took off running, closing in on the house. They'd been in the tree line surrounding the property.

I took slow, measured steps, my bare feet slapping on the parquet floor as I stepped off the cold metal. People moved away from me like I was projecting a repellent force, always an arm's length away.

The amiable smile never left my face, and I could see their nerves shattering to pieces. I kept walking, down the length of the hall and to the doors. Rushing feet in heavy boots came at me from the main house and a large group of guards appeared. My claws were out in an instant, and after the first two men fell with gaping wounds in their necks, the others turned tail and scattered.

I looked back at the baron, crouching behind his throne like a coward. "Be seeing you," I winked. Let him live every day in fear.

I broke into a run and tried to wrench open the front doors, but they were locked. I backed up and got a running start, crashing through them. They were more solid than I expected, and I wrenched my shoulder going through.

Excited yells drew my attention, and I saw my mates rushing over the lawn. I crashed into them with such momentum that we tumbled to the ground. There was no time for greetings, and I leaped to my feet, Gareth's yellow eyes and Andrus's red-rimmed irises fixating on the house behind me. People were pouring out onto the lawn, shouts and panicked cries echoing toward us.

The three of us turned and ran, seeking cover in the trees. I could already hear the horsemen mobilizing, heavy hooves drumming into the earth as they gave chase. The thicket of trees wouldn't provide cover for long, and it was a long way to the city.

"Ready to run?" I asked them with a grin.

"Let's go," they agreed.

Gareth and I quickly undressed and shifted, tossing our clothing at an annoyed Andrus and bounding ahead.

"How did I turn into your beast of burden?" he grumbled under his breath, but stuffed the balled-up clothing under his arm and took off after us, quickly gaining ground. I yipped at him as he took up his place on the other side of me and shot me a grin.

The horses had no hope of catching up to us like this. They fell behind until even my wolf ears couldn't hear them anymore. We kept running until the dawn light crept up over the city ahead of us.

CHAPTER FOURTEEN

Gareth

"We're not going to have much time. As soon as word gets back to the garrison, they're sure to kill Remi," said Meg, transforming into her human self and leaning forward on her knees to catch her breath. "Damn, that was a long way to run."

Andrus and I collapsed on either side of her, also struggling. "It certainly was," I said, pushing hair out of my sweaty face. I couldn't remember the last time I'd actually exhausted myself on a run.

"What are our options to get him out?" asked Andrus.

Meg's face fell. "It's locked down tight. His shackles are spelled, only able to be opened by the alchemist. They put me in his cell with him, and I couldn't find any vulnerabilities. To make matters worse, he doesn't want to be rescued."

My mouth fell open at the suggestion. "Are you sure?"

Meg nodded and heaved a sigh. "He was pretty damn direct about it. I couldn't believe it either. He tried to make up some excuse about the Titans having turned their backs on him, but the more I pressed him about it, the more it became clear he's just given up hope. I'm not sure if the three of us crashing in there to save him is going to bolster his spirits or simply make him angrier."

"He's always been a grouchy bastard, but he's never been a defeatist," said Andrus, curious.

"They've had him in there for five years," Meg said. She looked off into the distance. "He's covered in scars. There are two huge marks on his back, were they dug in and cut something off him." She blinked a few times. "I want to say they were wings, but I guess I'm not even sure what Remi is?"

"A gargoyle," supplied Andrus.

Meg paused. She sucked in her lips and chewed on them, like she was trying to conceal a smile. She ran her hands over her face, leaving dirt streaks in their wake before leaning her head on the wall behind her. "Of course he is."

Exhausted, strained laughter burst from her chest. She saw the horrified looks on our faces, but that only made her laugh harder. She sank down the wall until she was crouching low, knees tucked into her chest.

Andrus looked at me. "I don't get it."

I shook my head. "Meg?"

Tears were streaming down her face, but I could feel the pain and anxiety that accompanied her hysteria. It was a heady mix of emotion.

As her laughter silenced, she slapped her hands to her knees and stood, taking a deep breath. "One day soon, you too will see the irony of a gargoyle financing a cathedral." She shook her head with one more soft laugh and strode ahead.

"Where are you going?" I asked.

"To do something really stupid."

"I'm sorry, you want to what?" asked Andrus, face aghast. "I thought we were all on the same page that they were too dangerous. That we were trying to get away from them."

Meg just looked between us resolutely. "I know, and I'm completely in agreement. But what other choice do we have? The guards know exactly who we are. Or at least they know who I am. Doing anything else would take too long. Any minute a messenger could come along to deliver the baron's orders. Then they either kill him, or put him under even heavier guard."

"You're not thinking clearly. Maybe we should just take a minute and rest. You've been through a lot." Andrus was gripping her elbow, trying to draw her away, in the direction of our hiding place, but she wasn't having it.

"What if you try the same thing that you did with the tunnel?" I asked. "You said you had a much better grasp on reversing time, now. Would that be an option?"

"No. It would involve too many people, too large a place. Maybe someday, but right now I can't even begin to fathom how it would work without causing more problems than it solved." She looked at me appraisingly. "Unless you have some idea?"

In the corner of my mind, I could feel the strange being that was Time creep forward. It was intrigued by our conversation, but it simply pushed me away when I posed the question.

I frowned. "It seems to think we're not ready for that yet."

"Of course. Because why would any of this be easy?" said Meg, frustrated.

"Where's the fun in easy?" I asked. I'd intended to lighten the mood, but Andrus brought the reality crashing back down.

"I think it sounds like great fun not to have to call in the Hounds to help us."

We were approaching the garrison, and all still seemed quiet. The gates had been opened to allow for the first of the morning visitors. Without pause, Meg walked through the gates with us close behind. She held her head high, making periodic eye contact with the guards that we passed. Some of them did double-takes, but not one stood in our way. She continued into the main garrison block, pulling open a door like she knew exactly where she was going and had every right to be there.

I attempted to achieve the same amount of confidence that she was exuding, but to be honest, my nerves were getting the best of me. We were heading into the proverbial belly of the beast, and to help us escape, the plan as it stood was to hand ourselves over to even more foul creatures that were chasing us across time and space. Meg may have been confident that they weren't going to kill us, but would capture and being handed over to Belsioch be any better?

We were halfway down a long flight of stairs when the first alarm was raised. A handful of guards appeared at the top and bottom of the stairs, but without hesitation, Meg charged forward, bowling over several and attacking any that came after her. Andrus and I made quick work of the ones behind, sending their bodies tumbling down the stairs to land in a heap.

As we moved closer to the area that would be sealed off, preventing all magick from going in or out of that space, Meg tapped into time and sent out the call that would lead the Hounds directly to us. More running feet came in our direction, but they wouldn't make it in time.

Andrus swung the door to the chamber shut, and I helped him barricade it just as the sound of pounding fists hammered at it from the other side. Meg was searching the room and landed upon a set of keys hanging from the wall. She had to jump to reach them, and then she set to work trying each key in the lock.

The dull *snick* of the lock disengaging reached my ears, and I braced myself for what I was about to see. As the door swung open, my eyes strained to make out shapes in the gloom. Meg ushered us in and grabbed the keys before slamming it shut behind us.

The lock reengaged and I looked at Meg, eyebrows raised. "Did you intend for us to be locked in here?"

She pulled a face. "No, but now you won't have to hold the door closed when they make it through the other one."

Andrus spoke in the darkness. "So many ways this plan could still go wrong."

A rumbling, raspy voice issued from the corner of the room. "You truly don't listen, do you? And you brought your *mates* to slaughter as well."

A whole host of emotions ran through my head when I heard his voice, not the least of which was relief, maybe even happiness. But it was quickly overshadowed by the cruel tone, which only raised my ire. "Remi," I said, angling my body toward the source. "Try not to be a completely ungrateful bastard."

"Ungrateful? I am plenty grateful, brother, that we can see each other again before we die together." Spite dripped off his words. Chains rattled, and my vision finally adjusted to the darkness.

Andrus shuffled forward. "It's been a long time. I'd ask how you've been, but—"

Remi ground out a painful laugh. "Best years of my life. I don't know what you're talking about."

A crash startled me as the guards burst through into the main chamber. Footsteps pounded and fists battered against the iron door. Wrenching, pulling, shouts to find the keys. A smaller covering on a window cut into the door flipped back and a pair of sallow eyes peered in at us.

The eyes widened in surprise when they could see all four of us within the room and a low chuckle floated through the air, menacing and triumphant. "They've trapped themselves for us. These creatures really are stupid."

The commotion in the room stilled as they gathered in a tight group, shuffling for a position at the window to check for themselves. Sighs and relieved laughter was the prevailing noise before everything went to hell.

"On the contrary," said a soft voice that sent chills up my spine. My whole body tensed as I remembered what happened the last time these beings showed up. How quickly they'd set upon me. How fast I fell under their blades into complete oblivion.

I jumped when Meg's hand wrapped around mine before gratefully squeezing her fingers.

The voice continued. "It would seem they were actually clever. You men are the ones that are in quite a spot of bother."

I couldn't look away as the guards turned to face the new arrivals. They spread out and I could see the Hounds standing in the middle of the room, looking exactly like they did the first time I'd seen them. They were completely calm, not a trace of nervousness that they were outnumbered two to one by men twice their size.

The guards understood they were in the presence of true terror. They'd all fallen silent, furtive glances cast between each other their only movements. The pungent odor of urine made my nose wrinkle, and I could see a puddle forming at the feet of one. I pitied these men. They knew they were looking their death in the face, and there was absolutely nothing they could do to stop it.

There was a rush of wind and the wet, sudden noises of tearing flesh. Blood splattered around the room, splashing across every surface. And then it was done. The Hounds stood once again in the center, not a spot of blood on any of them. The still-twitching bodies of the guards surrounded them.

Rattling last breaths faded away, and then the beasts stepped forward. The woman reached her hand out and made a clawing motion in the air. The door began to groan and shake before it burst off its hinges and flew across the room. All three floated into the cell, and I heard a sharp breath from Remi as they surrounded him.

I clenched Meg's hand tighter. Gods, I hoped she was right about this.

One of the Hounds made a soft *tsk*-ing sound as they appraised the wounded gargoyle. "What have they done to you?"

Another said, "They call *us* monsters, but we don't cause pain for pain's sake." Three pairs of eyes turned on us after that statement, confirming that we'd heard them.

"Is that supposed to give us some kind of comfort?" asked Meg.

The Hounds grinned in unison. "We don't deal in comfort. We speak simple truths."

A loud clashing clapped through the small space as all the chains fell to the floor in a heap. Remi dropped onto his knees and then forward, his palms slapping against the flagstones. He took in a huge racking breath and for a brief moment, I worried that the sudden shift might cause irreparable harm to his already weakened body. I didn't know how much of the last five years he'd spent suspended from the ceiling, but even if it was a fraction of that time, the change had to have been shocking.

In the back of my mind, I could feel something nagging at me. An awareness of a different magick at work. A pressure was building around us, but I couldn't tell the source. Two of the Hounds were supporting Remi between them. In unison, they spoke. "Are you ready to go?"

"Where are you taking us?" Andrus asked.

"You already know." They were still speaking in their unholy chorus. If they could feel the magick building, they showed no sign.

There was a pulling sensation as the Hounds opened their own portal, and then... chaos.

Chapter Fifteen

Meg

Even though it had been my plan, I certainly hadn't expected it to go like it did. The magick of the sorcerers, or rather, the infernal chaos demons that were controlling them, was so pervasive and so powerful, its chokehold on this city was an ultimate possession. I knew that if creatures as strong as the Hounds stepped foot here, there would be repercussions. But I honestly had no idea how those infernal bastards would respond.

The room exploded and the entire garrison crumbled around us. Just before the walls collapsed inward, burying us under the rubble, we were all swept away. I was plenty accustomed to traveling through time and space, but this was unlike anything I'd ever experienced. It felt like I was being torn apart at the atomic level, fire raking over every inch of my body, every nerve ending. And then I was reassembled at the endpoint.

Everything went quiet.

I opened my eyes and stared around me blearily, noticing my companions were doing the same, except for Remi who was still unconscious. I did a double take. The Hounds had been transported as well, and they looked just as confused as we did. I wasn't sure if that scared me more, or less.

We were in some kind of underground chamber, ancient-looking stone pillars, more like a neolithic monument than a finely honed crafted column, ringed the room around us. There was grass beneath our feet, thick and healthy, despite all lack of sunlight. The walls were polished black obsidian, the mirrored surface uneven, distorting our images.

In the center, around which we were all gathered, was a massive stone altar, stained with dark splashes of blood. I could taste the copper on my tongue, and a faint smell of rot permeated the place.

Gareth and Andrus stepped close beside me. Remi was still lying unconscious on the ground, and I gasped as I got a better look at him in the bright firelight that lit the chamber.

His body was covered in the outline of those chains. Everywhere they touched, they'd burned into him, leaving chain-link scars over his entire body, covering the thick scars that had already been there when they'd hung him from the ceiling in the first place. The crude marks where they removed his wings with a saw were jagged and pulpy, bits of bone sticking out from gray flesh that looked like weathered and worn stone, standing out starkly against the rest of his skin. But I remembered those wounds being a lot flatter before.

Fresh blood trickled from one as I watched, and one of the bone shards twitched. "Oh, my gods," I whispered. His wings were trying to grow back. They must have kept removing them.

I couldn't even begin to imagine the agonizing pain that he must be in, all the time.

"Are we beneath the cathedral?" asked Andrus, kneeling beside Remi and checking for a pulse. Satisfied, he stood.

Gareth agreed. "Yeah, it seems like it."

Footsteps crushed the lush grass and all of us, including the Hounds, spun to face the noise. Four figures glided toward us. The Strangers that we'd seen with Father Montrose, now with airs of sinister anticipation about them. They were practically vibrating with excitement as they fixed me and my mates with a cruel smile.

Then they turned to the Hounds, and their expression changed to fury. The tallest of the group spoke. They all looked almost identical, just with slight differences in height.

"You dare come into my territory."

The Hounds, shaking off their uncertainty now that their enemy had a face, resumed their nonchalant attitude. "You'll have to accept our apology. We don't even know who you are." The man speaking flicked his gaze to us. "We'll take them and leave."

"You're not going anywhere."

"Belsioch is expecting them," said the Hound, simply.

The Stranger tilted his head back and laughed. "He has no power here."

The Hounds were not anticipating this reaction. They looked at each other, rolling their shoulders in anticipation of a fight. "Even if he doesn't, I'm still not sure you understand the gravity of the situation," said the woman. "This does need to turn nasty. Let us take them and leave. Otherwise, we'll be forced to kill you."

The Stranger let out a giggle, which was terrifying in itself, but then it turned into hysterical laughter, that crescendoed in a shriek. "The Hounds are no match for us."

Then the four figures began to split and multiply. In seconds, dozens of shadowy figures had splintered off from their main bodies and coalesced into solid shapes, tall humanoid creatures standing shoulder to shoulder. Features began to appear, twisted grins and sharp teeth. Giant eyes that were solid black, and hungry. Skin with the mottled, bruised look of a decaying corpse, shot through with bright green veins.

I backed up several paces, and my men stepped forward, but it annoyed me. When they'd done this before, putting themselves between me and danger, I thought it was sweet, protective. And that was still what they were doing. But I was so much stronger now. More confident.

I didn't need their protection. I needed partners in the fight.

And besides all that, if these things decided to attack us, there was little we could do. We'd be overwhelmed in a heartbeat, and we would only be able to hope that our deaths would be as quick. There were so many of them, all moving as if they were connected by one singular mind. Unlike the Hounds, who reminded me of triplets that were close enough to anticipate each others movements and thoughts, these creatures were all appendages of one entity.

Terror bubbled up. I could only think of one chaos demon that fit that description. What had I gotten us into?

"Legion," said one of the Hounds in a sharp hiss, confirming my fears.

My breath caught around my heart as it lodged in my throat. The Hounds were beings that more than likely weren't even born from our world. Now it seemed we were about to be witness to a battle between them, and the demon that other chaos demons told spooky stories about.

"Holy shit," I whispered.

"Accurate description," said Andrus, managing a tiny smile.

His joke helped me shake off the immediate shock and allowed me to settle back into fight mode. The Hounds were having a stare down with Legion and the silence was so still and uncomfortable that I shifted from foot to foot in a desperate attempt to ground myself. We just needed a chance to escape. Once they were distracted with each other, we might have a shot.

My mind went over everything I could remember about infernals. I didn't have much hope of remembering something that would be able to stop a chaos demon, but it kept my mind from devolving into wordless screaming.

All Strangers are tied tightly to the elements. We operate in all realms, above, below, and in between. The difference was that the Titans and the infernals could tap into primordial, raw energy, transmuting it for their needs. The Ætherim and fae dealt in energy that was produced by the natural world, bending it and shaping it as needed. One source was infinite, the other was not.

I always wondered if the Ætherim and their brethren out-numbered the Titans and infernal-kind so greatly as a way for the universe to balance things out.

I shook my head. That didn't help ease my fears at all, seeing as we were trapped in a small space with two seemingly limitless forces. We just needed them to forget about us for a second, so we could slip away and leave them to their battle. The end result wouldn't matter if we were far from here when it happened.

The Hounds were shifting their own forms, and I watched, horrified, as they grew in size, their limbs elongating, their spines curving, razor-sharp ridges of bone protruding outward. Their faces were grotesque—giant lamp-like eyes, jutting cheekbones and mouths that cut across the entire length of their jawline filled with several rows of teeth and a forked, slavering tongue.

Gareth and Andrus slowly herded me backward, and we surrounded Remi, still unconscious. Every direction was thick shadow beyond the pillars. The torchlight just seemed to cut off, devoured by the dark. I got the very real sensation that if we walked into those shadows, we'd never find our way back out again. The magick was oppressive, but I reached for the stream of time, nearly yelping in surprise when it answered.

When the Hounds had first crashed our party, I had connected to Andrus's mind and spoken to him that way. I have no idea how it happened, but I tried to do that now. Even with the seething creatures transforming before us, it was quiet enough for voices to carry.

Gareth caught me staring at him and jumped a bit. "What?" he asked.

I looked at Andrus and pointedly motioned from my head to his with the flat of my hand. "Remember?"

He stared at me in confusion only for a second before understanding lit his face. He returned my intense look, and Gareth was left staring between us without any clue what was going on.

I paid close attention to anything that felt different, hoping to pinpoint how this trick was done. There was a slight pressure behind my right eye that spread to my left and then centered. I might've described it as a minor headache, except that Andrus's voice sounded in my head.

Is it working? he asked.

I nodded, breathing a sigh of relief. Andrus turned to Gareth and attempted to bring him into our conversation, but it didn't seem to work. Finally, Andrus stabbed a finger right dead center of Gareth's forehead. I wasn't sure if it was because of frustration or some kind of trick that he was aware of that would allow Gareth to tap in to the mind-meld, but either way, it worked.

Gareth was about to angrily snap at Andrus, but the vampire stopped him. *Listen up, dummy.*

He was surprised, but quickly adjusted. *This is new*, his voice rumbled.

I can tap into the time stream.

Both men shot me a look.

Can we take him with us while he's unconscious? asked Gareth.

I nodded. *That won't be a problem. Once they're distracted, we go.*

Both men nodded and moved slowly toward Remi, ready to grab him.

The Hounds and Legion had reached the point of their argument where it was mostly teeth gnashing and growls. The many forms of Legion that had split off from the infernal swelled like a rising tide, preparing to strike.

Then the demon lunged, its grotesque bodies surging forward with one mind, flowing over the Hounds in a wave of ripping and tearing claws. The Hounds fought back with equal ferocity, tossing bodies left and right, crushing heads and splattering gore.

For every body they destroyed, Legion had two more, the scene before us devolving into a frenzy of blood and screeching.

One of the Hounds went sailing across the room, heading straight for the shadows, but it contorted its body in midair and grabbed a pillar, swinging itself around and hurling back toward Legion.

With the three of them ensconced in battle, surrounded by the many slobbering forms of their enemy, I reached out to time and pulled it toward us, urging Gareth to do the same. It was more responsive with him helping me, and the faster we could slip out of here the better.

Gareth and I both kept a firm grip on Remi's wrists, and Andrus wrapped his arms around me. I didn't know for sure if we could get separated during travel, but I wasn't willing to take the chance.

Just before we blinked out of that place, one of the Hounds turned and spotted us. It screeched and bounded toward us, but several of Legion's bodies jumped in front of it, trying to take it to the ground. A massive explosion of energy shook the chamber, and there was a blinding flash of light before we were swept away.

I picked a heading toward the next Desma—somewhere in Herculaneum—when we just... dropped out of the ether. And right back to the ceremonial chamber we'd just left.

Only this time, it looked much different.

Legion had been decimated. Its corpses lay everywhere, and the few that we're still standing were fusing back into a single form as we watched. The Hounds had also returned to the forms I was familiar with, gore and ichor dripping from their hands.

The beastly trio turned to us with their sickly smiles firmly in place. "You forgot something," said one, motioning to a place just below its collarbones.

What the hell were they talking about? I looked at the others, who seemed just as confused. And then my eyes lit on Remi, and the softly glowing lump on his chest.

Gareth and Andrus followed my gaze as I reached out and ran my hands over the shape.

"Handy, that. Returns the bearer to whoever holds the key." The Hound nodded to Legion. "That would be them." The trio stalked forward and surrounded us. The female reached down and dug into Remi's chest, pulling the stone from under his skin. It was attached by strands interwoven into his muscles. She tore it free with a wrenching pull and threw it in Legion's direction with a scowl.

"Time to go."

I caught one last sight of the infernal sinking back into the shadows. My plan had failed.

Chapter Sixteen

Death

"Incoming," I called. Bel looked over at me with annoyance.

"Do you mind?" he asked, raising his book.

"I thought you'd want to be ready for visitors."

Bel sat up and looked over to the center of the chamber, where the air was shimmering. The portal opened and the Hounds, accompanied by four, much worse-for-wear Strangers stepped through.

"Excellent!" shouted Bel, jumping to his feet. Meg looked terrified at his approach, and the mates standing on their own two feet jumped in front of her, launching themselves at Bel.

He swiped them aside easily. It was his turf, after all. He made the rules when he built this place.

The Hounds dropped the third and he fell to the floor, a gaping hole in his chest oozing blood. Their eyes fixed on me. "Our payment."

I met their gaze, unblinking.

Bel was tossing the four into their own cells. "Payment you'll receive after the job is complete. There are two more Desma." He looked at them as if seeing them for the first time. "What happened to you?"

Their annoyance was clear. "Slight problem with an infernal. Nothing we couldn't handle."

"Wonderful." Bel cast a glance in my direction. "Then you should be able to make quick work of rounding up the others. If you'll excuse me."

Since their contract was still pending, the Hounds reluctantly left, and Bel paced the room with glee as he observed his prizes. "Get comfortable. You'll be staying a while."

He left without a backward glance.

"Are you alright?" asked Meg.

"Perfectly fine, thank you," I answered. Awkward silence fell. "Oh, you weren't talking to me, of course. Forget I'm here."

"Who are you?" asked Meg.

Andrus gasped. "Death?"

I pointed at him with one finger while touching my nose with another. "Got it in one."

"Bel captured you too?" Meg's question was laced with hopelessness.

"Not the way that he thinks. But never mind me. You talk amongst yourselves."

I stepped back into the recesses of my cell and settled in, listening only to the murmur of their voices as they chatted.

Several hours later an excited gasp brought my attention around.

"He's awake!" said Meg.

Remi was indeed sitting up and getting his bearings.

"Where are we?" he asked.

"Belsioch has us," said Andrus.

Remi snorted. "Of course he does."

The door at the end of the chamber banged open and Bel strode in. "Good, you're awake. It's about time."

"Bel, please—" Meg began.

"Don't," he growled, rounding on her. "Not a word." He took up his pacing again. "I've been waiting for this moment for a long time. You're all going to regret not submitting when you had the chance. Now it will be so much worse. I've spent hours wondering how I'd kill each of you. I had thought that I'd make it a group event. Get all of you together and let my dear Megiste witness her mates dying before I finally put her out of her misery."

He stopped in front of Gareth's cell. "You are the first?"

Gareth stared back at Bel, pure, unbridled hatred radiating from him. "I am."

Bel opened the cell and pulled Gareth out, dragging him by the neck and slamming him flat into the wall next to Meg's cell.

"But then I thought, why wait?" Bel produced a knife and held it to Gareth's throat. "I think I'll kill them one by one and let Megiste live with the grief before I kill another." Gareth struggled, but Bel only laughed and pointed the knife at Meg. "You can sit here with the corpses of your lovers, waiting to see who the Hounds will bring to the slaughter next."

"No!" Meg screamed, lunging against the bars of her cell, reaching for her mate.

Bel swiped the knife across Gareth's neck and the man flinched, but didn't make a sound. His killer looked up at Meg with a triumphant sneer. Only when he saw her look of confusion and relief did it falter.

Bel looked back at Gareth, whose neck was perfectly unharmed. "What?" he spat. He tried cutting Gareth again, and when that didn't work, he stabbed him multiple times. But the blade just wouldn't cooperate, not once penetrating the skin.

"What is happening!" Bel asked, foaming at the mouth in his fury. His eyes turned on me and I smiled, Mr. Amicable.

"Troubles?" I asked. I looked at Gareth and back at the fuming god still poised with his impotent blade. "Looks like you need a sharper knife."

"You." He threw the knife, and it embedded itself cleanly into the wood of a gaudily upholstered settee. He stalked over to my cell and reached through the bars. I made no move to stop him from grabbing the front of my shirt and pulling me toward him.

"What did you do?"

I feigned surprise. "Nothing at all. Like you said, I'm helpless to do anything from in here."

Bel jerked his fist, smashing my face against the bars. I only laughed.

"What did you do?" he repeated, smashing me against the cold iron but doing no damage.

"Maybe it's your strength." I laughed harder. "It feels like you're giving me a massage."

Bel howled with rage and released me. He picked up another weapon, striking Gareth with it repeatedly before throwing it aside for another. When that didn't work, he threw Gareth back in his cell and pulled Andrus to the center of the chamber. He tried the same thing, attacking Andrus with everything he could get his hands on. And none of it worked.

Flame was billowing from Bel's shoulders, rage etched in every feature. He shed his human guise, taking on his godly form, but it made no difference.

The room filled with the heat of his anger, and he finally turned his attention on Meg. He didn't even bother putting Andrus back in his cell before grabbing Meg and throwing her across the room. Andrus rushed to break her fall, catching her easily in his arms.

I applauded. "Good form. That's true chivalry right there."

Bel flung out his hand, sending a blast of magick in my direction. It seared across the front of my cage, curling in waves onto the ceiling and leaving scorch marks and cracks in its wake.

"Why won't they die?" he screeched. "Why won't they die!"

"Beats me. Maybe you should find a reaper to help you. I hear they can handle things just fine on their own."

"No. Confining you doesn't stop death from happening. The world will continue functioning as it always has without you in it. You're a figurehead only. The only thing that would be disrupted is the order, the organization. You're only around because the reapers can't tell their ass from a hole in the ground, and need to be told constantly what to do."

"I wouldn't put it quite so crassly as that. You're right. Death will happen exactly as it always has, with or without me." I cocked my head. "But I still command the very essence of it. It does what it's bidden by me, and if I say somebody's off-limits, they're off-limits."

"This isn't going to delay me handing you over to the Hounds," said Bel. "Stop playing these games!"

"The Hounds were never a factor here. Not truly. To you, they might be. And they will certainly be angry with you when

I am nowhere to be found as they come to claim their prize. But my goal here has always been different."

Bel was staring, his anger leaving him in an apoplectic fit, too furious to speak. So I filled the silence. "I don't like bullies." I smiled. "They've always rubbed me the wrong way. Everyone is equal in the eyes of death, but for some reason, they think they're different. They think they're better. That they can escape what's coming for them. And when those bullies have such an extreme amount of power, oh," I sighed, "that just rankles me." My smile fell away.

"I've been watching you for a very long time. I always made it a point to never choose sides. Because like I said, everyone is equal. But you, Bel, have made me change my mind. After all, evil is only allowed to persist when good folk do nothing. I tried to stay neutral, but I'd also fancy myself a decent being. Maybe not good. Good is boring, and I've always loved a delightful shade of morally gray."

Bel's furious stare was faltering. A tick of uncertainty twitched at his left eye.

"I can no longer stand idly by and watch you continue to be a complete and utter disgrace to the Ætherim. I don't know if your long years have finally sent you over the edge into insanity. It happens to the best of us. Or maybe you've always been a little crazy, but compared to everyone else you fit right in. And where the other gods either found balance or destruction, you just kept getting worse, and were lucky enough to have escaped from the forces that would've sought to end you."

Bel sneered. "What are you going to do? Kill me yourself?"

I shook my head. "That's not how this works. I don't kill people personally. That would be very blatantly choosing sides.

No." I paused, watching the relief flood Bel's face. "I'm just here to put a finger on the scales."

His eyes widened in alarm as I casually gripped the bars in my hands, pouring death and decay into the iron, watching it rust and flake, and fall away.

"Anyone that seeks to conquer death"—I scoffed—"is a weak"—I took a step forward—"terrified"—another step—"sniveling, worthless, powerless, simpering, incompetent... did I already say powerless?" I paused and glanced at Meg, who nodded. I shrugged. "I'll say it again anyway. Powerless, idiotic fool." My last step landed me right in front of Bel.

"I won't kill you. And right now, these four aren't strong enough to do it. But I will make sure they become that way. And they will tear you apart, and I will watch, and love every minute of it."

I whispered. "Death is coming for you. Have no doubt. But in the meantime." I slammed my fist dead center of Bel's chest, unleashing just enough power to drain half his life force and send him hurtling across the room to land in an unconscious heap.

I spoke to him, even though the lights were out, and nobody was home. "Consider the scales tipped, you sorry son of a bitch."

The silence that followed was tense. I blinked and peered around at the four chosen, my signature slow smile returning. "Damn, that felt good."

I made my way over to Gareth's cell and then Remi's, following the same process, dissolving the lock like I'd done to my bars. As soon as he was free, Gareth retrieved the knife and stalked over to Bel standing over him. "Let's just kill him now. Be done with it."

I shook my head. "That's not going to work, I'm afraid. Even at half capacity, he's still a god. You are not."

"A beheading will kill anything," growled Gareth, but his stance eased as he knew his words for false.

"Didn't you say that you'd ensure we would be the ones to kill him?" asked Meg.

"I did. And I said I'd prepare you for it. As it stands, you're not ready. Go ahead and stab him if it makes you feel better, but—"

Gareth plunged the knife directly into Bel's heart and left it there, returning to Meg's side and sweeping her up in his arms. Remi watched with a sullen, closed-off expression.

"Was all of that true?" she asked.

I tilted my head. "Mostly. There were a few more insults I wanted to add, but I ran out of steps."

They made an odd sight. The wolf holding Meg in his arms, the vampire clapping him on the back as they huddled together, and the odd gargoyle standing a few feet away. Not sure who Remi thought he was fooling. It was obvious how badly he wanted to be part of them, but wouldn't let himself give in.

They still didn't know quite what to make of me, unsure if they should be afraid. "Why don't I put you out of your misery right now?"

They all paused and stared at me in horror. I laughed, delighted at my own unintentional joke. "Not quite what I meant. My apologies. I'll give you answers without making you wait."

Sighs of relief all around. "I am sick and tired of Belsioch's actions. And I've been keeping an eye on your little group, ever since it became clear that you were the ones that would not only put a stop to him permanently, but you also have the best chance at truly freeing the Titans." I grinned. "And that is something I would very much like to see."

Meg spoke, imploring Gareth to put her down. Ah, youth. Reminded me of when I was a spry young fellow of only three-thousand years and in love for the first time.

"So you're offering help?"

I bowed deeply at the waist. "At your service." I held up a finger. "To an extent." I took a seat on an overstuffed cushion. Gods, this man loved tacky furniture. I batted at a couple of errant tassels. "But I must be clear, my help doesn't come for free."

"What would you want in return?" Andrus asked.

"There's a little project I'm putting together, gathering up a team." I left it there, wanting their curiosity to win out.

They all shared looks and there were a few furtive whispers before Andrus took up the lead once again. "And what would you be using this team for?"

I shrugged. "This and that."

Remi spoke up. "We're going to need a better explanation than that."

Meg rounded on him with a horrified look but my smile never wavered. "It's quite all right. I would be extremely concerned if you didn't ask follow-up questions. Although I'm still not going to give you a straight answer."

"Will you at least give us some idea?" asked Gareth.

"I assure you, I'm not trying to keep secrets. I'm not sure myself where this is going, just yet. The best I can do is to refer back to my perfectly timed, scathing last words to Bel. I mean to tip the scales. But in order not to choose sides, I need a team. One that will keep me objective." I looked directly at Remi. "Speak up, if they think I'm making a wrong turn. People who aren't afraid to question my motives. I'm tired of sitting on the sidelines."

"Will it do any good? To have people around that will question you?" asked Remi. "You could easily overpower any of us, destroy us with a thought. It's all well and good to say that you want oversight, so you can keep a clear head and a clean conscience, but it's another thing entirely to actually listen when people call you out. You are a supreme being of primordial essence. People like us mean nothing to you because we cannot hope to challenge your power."

He did have a point, I could admit that. "You'll just have to take my word for it." I patted the cushion, foregoing my attempts at making it comfortable. "But if it makes you feel any better, if you succeed in your mission, you will have quite a few equally powerful beings that will owe you a debt. And while they are my friends, I don't think they would hesitate to stomp me into oblivion if I became a power-hungry twat."

Remi shrugged. "As good a way as any of getting out of a contract."

"No contracts here, friend. Too much paperwork, never cared for it. It's a simple agreement."

"What about the Hounds?" asked Meg.

"Yes, well, I suggest you hurry on and find the rest of your mates. They are still searching for them, but it won't take them long."

"How do we stop them?" Gareth asked.

"That is a very specific problem, and I'm afraid me and one other person are the only ones who know the answer. And it will stay that way. However, if you should run across them again, send up a flare. Be there in a jiff."

"What's a jiff?" asked Remi.

Andrus snickered and grinned at Meg wickedly. "We need to get you two bonded."

Meg flushed a deep red and glanced at me apologetically, but I shook my head. "Don't be embarrassed. I know how it works."

Far from alleviating her mortification, she turned beet red. She laughed, burying her face in her hands. "Okay," she said, voice muffled, "let's move on to another subject, please."

I'd caught sight of Remi's back only briefly, and motioned for him to turn. Confused, he did as I asked before quickly turning back around to face me.

"A nasty thing, that." His face darkened, but he didn't reply. "I can restore your wings for you."

I thought for sure he would say yes, but he surprised me. "No. They'll grow back on their own. It's already started."

I blinked. Was I saying those words right? "I'm offering to alleviate the wait. I can restore them right now without pain."

"That's very generous of you, but I'm declining."

Gareth turned to him. "Why would you pass up that chance? Given how our luck usually goes on these missions, having somebody on our team with wings," he looked at Meg, "that could fly *our mate* out of danger, would be extremely helpful."

"You've all managed just fine so far," he said, crossing his arms to end the argument.

"What is wrong with you?" Andrus asked. "You've been nothing but a sullen bastard since we pulled you out of that prison. I saw your wings tacked to a wall. Three sets. You want to go through that pain a fourth time? You are not proving anything to anyone. You're being an obstinate fool."

"That's my choice." Remi turned away, wandering aimlessly around the room and ignoring the glares from his fellows.

"You—" began Gareth, but Meg put a hand on his arm.

"It's his choice," she said firmly. "He hasn't gotten to make a choice for himself in at least five years. Let him have this one."

"But he's putting you in danger. He's putting all of us at needless risk," said Andrus.

"He wasn't wrong when he said we managed just fine so far. We have. And we'll have to do so for a bit longer. We'll be okay."

I grinned. She was already proving to be a diplomat, and a great choice on my part. And they *would* be fine, if I had my way.

I was far too close to actualizing my idea to see it crumble now. Even if I had to call in favors or additional help. Hell, even if I had to make further personal appearances, I would do everything in my power to see them through to the end. But the road they had to take was not for the fainthearted. There was no shortage of courage among them, but I knew they would all be tested to their limits.

"Do you have an answer for me?" I asked.

They spoke briefly among themselves, minus Remi's input. Andrus nodded. "We have an agreement."

I clapped my hands together. "Excellent. Now, how about we get you to your next destination? I just got a significant energy boost. I'd be more than happy to send you myself so you can save your strength."

With one last disgusted look at Bel, Meg nodded. Remi joined the team but still insisted on staying an arm's length away. That was going to be a fun issue for them to work out.

"Ready?" Without waiting for an answer, I clapped my hands sharply.

And they were gone.

CHAPTER SEVENTEEN

Meg

Death had given us more than just an express travel pass. When we landed, we were in a cave and dressed in time-appropriate clothing.

"I'm already liking our new partnership," I said. "Anytime I can land and not be immediately threatened by an angry horse or a mob—"

"Or the gods of nightmares," said Gareth.

I nodded. "It's a good day."

The cave was situated on a rocky cliff, the ocean roaring around us. A small but thriving city was in the distance, alive with activity.

"Welcome to Herculaneum," I said.

Finding a place to settle in and call a home base was going to be more difficult than we anticipated. The city was packed with people, not a single abandoned or out-of-the-way place in sight. We'd settled instead on another cave closer to the city.

Andrus had gone to scout the area and do a little thieving while Remi headed toward the beach. What he really needed was the ear of one of his brothers, but he was still too weak to keep up with Andrus, and Gareth had done nothing but display open contempt for him.

Gareth and I had been wandering and gathering driftwood and beach grass to burn, as well as scouting the area for hunting potential. The cave was quiet when we returned.

"We've all suffered and have seen things that we wish we could forget," he fumed. "What makes him think he's entitled to act like this?"

"He's not doing it to be contrary," I said gently. "Think about where you were at before I found you. You'd almost given up hope. You thought the Titans had abandoned you, or at least that the plan had failed. Andrus felt the same. Now multiply that by being locked in a dark hole, without anyone to talk to except for the people that are there solely to hear your screams. Just waiting to die, completely cut off from everyone you cared about. Knowing that they'll never find out what happened to you."

Gareth sighed and sat heavily. "When you put it that way."

I sat next to him and leaned on his shoulder. "Give him a chance. I think he's keeping himself distant because he doesn't want to get attached. He's anticipating all of it being torn away from him again."

"Well, now I feel like a jerk." He wrapped his arm around me. "I'm glad we finally have some time alone. I've been wanting to get something off my chest."

I moved to sit in Gareth's lap, the familiar circle of his arms enclosing me as he nuzzled into my neck, breathing in my scent.

"Being away from you is unbearable, even for a short time." He kissed the bite mark he'd left on my shoulder. "I tried to convince myself I was devoted to you because of my duty. The oaths I took to the Titans, the promises I made to protect you. But you had my heart since we met. I never knew I could love someone so much."

I twisted to the side and melted against him, snuggling close, looping my arms around his shoulders.

"My wolf is still fighting me on this, but I am trying. Now with Remi in the mix, and either Felix or Hadi joining shortly." He paused. "I'm apologizing in advance. I hope I don't get into an alpha battle, especially with Hadi, but—"

I put my hand on his chest. "This will take a lot of adjustment. We just need to be honest, even when it hurts. But I would like to point out that—"

Gareth covered my lips with his own. When we came up for air he said, "Don't say I told you so."

I tilted my face up, searching for his lips, suddenly desperate to be consumed by him. His kiss was hot and frenzied as the last of our anxiety transformed into passion.

"I told you so," I whispered.

Gareth's arms tightened around me as he nipped my lip and his tongue swept through my mouth. He lifted me and set me on my knees, tearing my dress over my head in one swipe and doing the same with his own clothes. His mouth closed over my nipple and my back arched as his teeth grazed the hard bud while his hand moved south.

His fingers spread me open and brushed against my clit, his knuckle rubbing in tight circles and eliciting whimpers from me. I reached for his cock and stroked the soft skin, feeling him stiffen beneath my touch.

I reached between my legs and gathered my arousal on my fingers before continuing to stroke him, leaning down and swiping my tongue across his tip. His low moan echoed through the cave.

His arms wrapped around me again and laid me gently on my back. Gareth nestled between my legs, his gigantic frame straining my hips as I wrapped my legs around him. He lined up at my entrance and paused, looking into my eyes with tenderness and stroking my face.

He kissed me with a consuming attentiveness before pushing slowly into me, stretching me as I mewled, clawing at his back. It was torturous, this slow pace, my walls expanding and pulsing around his cock until he bottomed out. He stayed there, unmoving as we panted, still running gentle fingers over my cheek and jaw.

"I love you," he whispered.

I pulled his face to me for another kiss. "I love you."

The purest smile I'd ever seen from him lit up his face, and he snuck one more kiss before he moved in long, languid strokes.

I clenched my thighs around him, urging his movements, levering my hips up to meet him and pulling him deeper on every inward thrust. The first pulse of pleasure zipped through my body, leaving me lightheaded.

His pace quickened and I gasped as I neared climax. Our breathing synchronized as we groaned in tandem, our bond singing with mutual pleasure.

The tension ratcheted too high, and I felt as tightly strung as Apollo's bow. Gareth drove deep and I screamed my release, his own following after a few more thrusts, the warmth of being filled sending my orgasm to its peak and taking my breath away. Mouth agape in a silent scream, my back arched off the floor and Gareth slow stroked me through it, bringing me down gradually.

He rolled to the side and brought me with him. I teased my fingers through the thick hair on his chest before resting my palm over his racing heart.

We'd just gotten re-dressed when Andrus returned. "Remi isn't back yet?" he asked.

"No. He must still be at the beach."

Gareth stood. "We should probably go find him. I owe him an apology."

The beach was mostly deserted except for a shape sitting shoulders-deep in the ocean.

"Is he letting the salt water bathe his wounds?" Andrus asked.

Remi noticed us coming and stood, the water droplets catching the sun and sparkling as they scattered. He made his way back to his pile of clothes and pulled them on before we could get a good look at his back.

Gareth frowned. "How are you planning on hiding your wings? It won't be long before they're noticeable through your clothing. Until that part of you is healed, you can't incorporate them into your human body."

I touched his arm, and he grimaced. "I'm sorry. I came down here to make amends, not make it worse."

Remi nodded but didn't speak. Gareth was about to say something else but there was a rumble underneath my feet and I almost pitched to the side, losing my balance before Remi caught me. Our entire world shook, and it was almost thirty seconds before it stopped.

"Was that an earthquake?" I asked.

"Sure felt like one," cursed Andrus. "The one thing I never missed about home."

Gareth shook his head. "But doesn't an earthquake in these parts usually mean—"

"We might have a problem," grumbled Remi.

We all turned, staring at the towering volcano belching thick, black smoke.

"Oh, for fuck's sake," I sighed.

Coming Soon

The Primordial Embers Series Continues...
Look for a new release EVERY MONTH, six novellas in total!
Look for Book 4 in the series September 24th, 2024

The Death's Left Hand Series:
Death's Left Hand Book 3 – October 8th, 2024
Death's Left Hand Book 4 – November 12th, 2024

Visit gwydionroyce.com or follow @gwydionroyce on instagram and facebook for the latest updates!